the

LIBRARY

of

EVERYTHING

HUNTER TERRELL

Cover design copyright © 2024 by Design by Definition
daniellefine.com

Published by Paper Angel Press
paperangelpress.com

ISBN 978-1-962538-65-7 (Hardcover)

FIRST EDITION

10 9 8 7 6 5 4 3 2 1

"Friend" said the Spirit. *"Could you, only for a moment, fix your mind on something not your-self?"*

C.S Lewis, *The Great Divorce*

the

LIBRARY

of

EVERYTHING

1

THE LIBRARY
AND ITS CHARACTERS

L ILY FOUND HERSELF in the Library in a dream; or maybe it wasn't a dream. Either way—she knew that the experience was something more than imaginary, but less than real. A short, brown-eyed young woman with a blue-green knitted beanie that she had worn most every day since childhood, Lily sensed the strangeness of her situation, but whatever impulse might normally bring panic was absent in this moment, so Lily did what she would normally do in a dream (or in a not dream)—she walked around, looking left and right, with her arms folded.

The Library was a liminal sort of place. It was at once a place known from childhood and also a place very foreign. It didn't feel like it was somewhere; it wasn't its own location. It seemed … in between. It was a building to be sure, though it felt more like an elevator, or a road, or a hallway. But the Library was none of these things— it was a Library; not unlike ones you've seen before, with dark blue carpet, warm lamps on the walls, wooden desks and chairs, and of course, bookshelves. Tall, and endless, and full of books.

As she walked, Lily looked around the tall shelves, full of hundreds, no, thousands of books. Maybe hundreds of thousands. All of them looked much alike— save for the titles on the spines. Some of the titles were very plain and academic, like *Mt. Sumdum*, while other books had quaint names such as *Andre's Picket Fence in Salento*. Other titles were quite nonsensical, take *Fujunishalikertyopica 37th Neverdone* for example …

One book in particular caught her eye. The title on the spine read *Tranquil Beach*. She stopped and cautiously reached up toward it, pulling it out of its sacred place with one hand, revealing a midnight black backstop to the otherwise warm wooden shelf. She held the book in front of her face for examination. The first thing she noticed upon removing it from its shelf was the weight— she felt as though she shouldn't be able to lift it—yet she could easily. The second thing she noticed was the size. On the shelf she was sure that it was the same size as all the other books—quite large and thick, yet holding it now, it seemed like a reasonably sized novel. But the real magic was not in the size nor the shape.

She parted the book to expose a random page she felt was about the middle, and what she read there was quite unlike any book she had ever read before. Lily had always loved reading, but what she read here seemed to skip the active processing part of her brain and immediately enter the long-term memory part of her brain, giving her a strange sense of *deja-vu*. She was reading, for sure, and could recount with some accuracy what she was reading, but could detail no specific words or sentences, or even letters for that matter—she couldn't even be certain that the book was in English, save for the fact that she could understand it.

She read about Tranquil Beach, and a hungry seagull, and beautiful waves … She had a sense that what she was reading was real; it certainly was no fiction novel. The book described scenes with too much detail and no discernible plot. It seemed random and chaotic, much like the world she knew, not the books she knew. She closed the book and shuddered, replacing it on its shelf. Lily had always been easily unsettled, and bad experiences had a way of sticking with her. She tried to shake it off, and kept walking.

The first sound Lily was aware of was the soft scratching of her Chuck Taylor's on the worn blue carpet tile. Very painfully conscious of her footsteps echoing through the otherwise seemingly desolate Library halls, Lily refused to call out the obligatory, trepid "Hello?" into the void, for she had a small voice, and she used it sparingly, only when social expectations were strong enough to force it from her. Fortunately, storytelling conventions were upheld, as Lily heard the stereotypical call ring out through the Library—from a middle-aged, East-Coast woman, by the sound of it.

"HalllloOOooo …" the nasal voice called out.

The social obligation getting to Lily— "… hel— *throat clear* hello?"

The clack of heels coming around the corner revealed that the two characters had been divided by a single row of bookshelves, merely one hall apart. Jane hustled around the corner toward Lily. Jane looked like she used to be pretty, before she had put her body through all the drugs, and men, and procedures. Her face was pulled tight, caked with makeup, overly shiny and orange, and her eyebrows were tattooed permanently pointy. But her age was given away by her arms—the saggy, spotted skin that clung to bone, and the wrinkled hands. Jane wore big hoop earrings and a bright pink top with white slacks. She had long acrylic nails, and she carried a tiny matching purse. You probably wouldn't recognize her, but she was a famous popstar in some circles.

Jane was smacking gum. (It is unclear whether she had begun her journey in the Library already chewing it, or if the first thing she did in the Library was put in a stick of gum) "What's going on? Why am I in a libary?" she questioned Lily, who shrugged.

The two looked at each other, and then around at their surroundings, neither being quite sure what they were looking for. Lily had never in her life taken any psychedelic drugs, but she wondered if somehow this was some kind of a trip. Jane had done plenty of psychedelics, but was fully convinced that she had been kidnapped, or was perhaps being pranked. The impossibleness of the Library was lost on her, and she was sure there were hidden cameras, and that the person responsible for this would reveal themselves soon.

Jane pulled the latest generation of iPhone out of her purse. "I don't got any signal in here. You swear you're not in on this?" Lily nodded fervently. "Well I have things to do. HALLLLOOOOOOO!!" she shouted again into the air, her voice so shrill as to make Lily wince.

The Library responded with a long silence.

"We could ask the librarian," Lily mumbled.

"The libarian??"

"Well, yeah … every library has a librarian … right?" Lily was sure there had to be a librarian but wasn't sure how she knew. It just felt like one of those obvious realities about the world that needn't be observed to be believed.

"Well, someone did this. Let's go find 'em," Jane conceded.

And so, Jane and Lily continued in the direction they had been going before running into each other. They walked down a couple more halls, around a few corners, to the desk to talk to the librarian. The librarian greeted the two as they approached.

"Welcome Jane, Lily, I've been expecting you! Do you know what books you are looking for?"

Lily let Jane answer first. "What is this place?" But before having her question ignored, the librarian fixed her expectant gaze upon Lily—"Umm … No. I like books, but I don't really know what this place is, I guess."

"It's the Library. It has literally everything."

"Everything?"

"Not like *Hamlet* or *Moby Dick* or *Twilight* or any of the books you know …"

"So you just have, like, non-fiction, then?"

"Well, not exactly. The Library doesn't have books like that either. See, it's—"

"Where is this place?" Jane demanded.

"It isn't anywhere, it's kind of everywhere. It's not a place within a bigger place—it's just the Library."

Jane rolled her eyes at the librarian's unhelpful answer, but before she could get another question out, the librarian rose from her desk abruptly—

"Let's go find the others."

"Others?"

•   •   •

Elsewhere in the Library was Christopher, a middle-aged man with a greying beard, whose felted vest struggled to restrain his hefty gut. Chris was holding a fishbowl—in that fishbowl was a goldfish. Chris didn't own a fish, but he now looked one in the eye. It was small and looked exactly like any goldfish you might see at a fair, except it was a vibrant purple. Chris had never looked a fish in the eye, and was surprised at the intelligence he saw there, in the thing gulping water from the plain glass bowl. This fish's name was Barnacles; remember Barnacles the goldfish—he will be important later.

Chris came from money but prided himself in dressing modestly—below the vest, a pressed plaid shirt was tucked into a simple pair of trousers, accompanied by older, but well-kept, leather shoes. Chris' attentions were divided by his surroundings—he looked around at the Library and marveled.

He sensed he wasn't alone, and so he somewhat quickly and quietly carried the goldfish bowl around the bookshelf behind him, (after having briefly assessed his immediate vicinity for any suitable place to set the goldfish and finding nowhere) scanning left and right for signs of life. Just a few dozen shelves down the hall was a figure sitting on the floor against a wall of books.

"Howdy," Chris announced his presence as he approached the floor-sitter.

He was an average-looking young guy with messy hair. He was in jeans and a Captain America t-shirt. He introduced himself lamely as Sam. Sam came off as the sort of fellow who lived his life as though he were just waiting for it to be over. He worked at a general store, lived with an equally lame roommate, played video games too much … And he, too, found himself in the Library.

"You wouldn't be keen as to our whereabouts, now, would you?" Chris questioned Sam, who shrugged.

Chris scratched at his beard with his free hand, perplexed. "Well golly, I must have gotten lost."

"I think, perchance, you've been found," said the librarian, appearing from around a corner, being followed by the two girls from earlier, Lily and Jane. Just as a third, new character also approached from a distance, having been drawn to the noise of conversation.

This woman joining them now was named Elizabeth—who was perhaps thirty? Mother of three, she appeared young and healthy, with a seriousness about her. She looked like your mom looks in old photos, warm and classic and purposeful. Elizabeth had a certain tiredness you could catch a glimpse of in her eyes every now and again when she thought no one was watching. She had wandered into Jane and Lily and the librarian and Sam and Chris, (and the goldfish), and was, for the moment, silently taking in the shock of such a bizarre scene.

"Oh, there you are, Liz," said the librarian, acknowledging Elizabeth's arrival.

Liz squinted. "Please don't call me tha–hey, wait, how do you know my name?"

The librarian pursed her lips and stretched her eyes to the left, avoiding the question, and soon was saved by the bell of Chris' further questioning.

Chris was surprised at the sudden appearance of an entire ensemble (he certainly wasn't the only one confused). He questioned, hopeful for some clarification on matters—

"How did you ladies get here?"

"The same way you did, silly," the librarian remarked.

Chris wasn't particularly flattered at being called silly, but he could tell that this librarian was somehow privy to information, and so, desperate for answers, he asked, "And just how might that be?" The entire group was quiet in anticipation of the librarian's response.

"You didn't get here—you just are here."

This was the final straw for the group, thoroughly fed up with the librarian's non-answers, and they all erupted in angst about their situation.

Sam shoved his hands into the pockets of his jeans and mumbled things like, "I don't know, man …"

Jane clicked her nails and snorted things such as, "I don't have time for this; I got places to be."

"Are my kids here?" asked Elizabeth, to which the librarian reassuringly shook her head.

Looking around at the vast multitude of books, Lily asked, "What kind of books are these? Is it … like a giant encyclopedia?"

Christopher bellowed out the loudest—"You have better give us some answers, missy!"

The librarian would quiet everyone so she could explain, finally, the nature of the Library.

"Listen. This Library is unlike any library you know. This Library contains the whole of everything. Everything. Look at that section over there. That section, which stretches to near-infinity, is for drops of water. Every water-drop has a book of its story—the ocean it came from, the clouds it travelled in, the flowers it will water, the cheeks it's rolling down in tears, the dinosaurs that drank it up and peed it out … And that other section is for trees, from seed to timber to dining room chairs. When and where and why it was planted, the animals that lived in it, children that climbed it, its offspring, the man that cut it down, and ultimately how it will be burned and sent to the sky in smoke. And those subsections are for the leaves of those trees, and the subsections under those are for the cells those leaves are made of, and under that is the carbon atoms making up those cells … One of my favorite sections is that one; it's for stars. I promise, if you look, you will find a couple hundred billion trillion books, one for every star. And each of those books will have a near infinite number of pages—somewhere under "S" is Sirius, whose book tells the whole story of how that star was born, the planets it has fostered, the asteroids it has consumed, the wonders it has witnessed, and how, after a long and full life, it will go out in a blaze of glory. Every rock has a book about the volcano it came from and the shoes it's been stuck in. Every flower, every dog, every dust mite, every galaxy … and every person that ever is or was or will be has a book containing the whole truth of their past, present, and future. Whatever is in those books is truth. This is the story of everything."

Sam stared open-jawed and wide-eyed. Chris furrowed his brow. The group was in wonder and some disbelief, except Jane, who had been tapping her foot and rolling her eyes around with her arms crossed. As soon as there was a break in the librarian's exposition, she popped off.

"Sister, I can't be here. Do you even know who I am? I gotta get back right now cuz my manager is supposed to tell me how Grooveyard Records liked my demo! This is my next big break! I have to be there!"

Christopher raised his eyebrow at the diva. "Well, lady, if the librarian is to be believed, you wouldn't need to go home at all to receive your news—supposedly there's a book around here with your name on it that tells it all!" Christopher gestured sarcastically at the books around them.

"I have a book about me?" she asked what everyone was thinking.

The librarian replied, "I just told you about an endless Library teeming with knowledge and art and story itself, everything that ever is or was or will be, and your first question is about your own book?"

The group paused for a minute, and looked around at one another, before nodding unanimously. The librarian's expression was a mix of understanding and disappointment.

"Of course you all have a book—everyone does. These books define and reflect reality as you know it—"

"And my book got the future in there? Some Gypsy Voodoo thing gonna tell me what the label say?"

"I don't think you'll like what you read," the librarian responded solemnly.

"You're gonna tell me they don't sign me? Funny. They tell me I'm a wizard, too?"

The librarian was offended. "I'm serious. This place is magical. These books tell the truth. Read one and see."

"It seems like it could be true," Christopher interjected. "There seems to be more to this place than meets the eye. If this isn't all just a dream, then we each are here quite supernaturally ..." Christopher developed his thoughts as he spoke. "This could actually be quite the opportunity!" he said, considering the profound implications of such a library.

Jane's sass was knocked down a peg. "So, I'm supposed to believe that this chick knows I ain't signing?"

Everyone turned to the librarian, each formulating the same realization independently. Lily recalled her experience reading one of the books, and believed what the librarian was saying. Elizabeth was the first to speak out. "Hey, you keep talking like you know us ... How did you know my name earlier? How do you know me?"

The librarian kicked at the carpet bashfully and put her arms behind her back like a shy schoolgirl.

"You've read my book, haven't you!" Elizabeth accused triumphantly on behalf of the group.

"Well, more like skimmed, you couldn't really read a whole book. I read about all of you before you came here."

"That's a bold claim, missy. Can you prove it?" Challenged Christopher.

"Your uncle's name is Ronald Albury, and his birthday was the fifth of November."

"I don't think that's his birthday," Chris hesitated.

"You don't know because you're a bad nephew," the librarian retorted. "Elizabeth, your youngest son just learned how to walk, and sometimes you worry about the day when you'll pick him up and set him down for the last time and never hold him again. Sam, you carry a Polaroid picture of a girl named Beatrice in your wallet. I bet you have it on you right now. Jane, you won't get this record deal like you haven't gotten the last four. Lily, your dad gave you that hat when you were thirteen and you've worn it almost every day since. And, Barnacles," the librarian said, leaning down towards the fishbowl in Christopher's arms, "you have got to be the most peculiar fish there ever was." The librarian's evidence was sufficient, and agitating.

"What is my story like?" "What happens?" "Do I make it?" The group erupted. Elizabeth was asking about her kids, Sam was asking about his girlfriend, Jane was confounded and Christopher, having the loudest voice, asked about his inheritance. The librarian chose silence, not having answers any of them would like.

Chris couldn't bear ambiguity. "Tell me if I get it or not!" (This being a reference to an inheritance from his uncle's will, about which he had been fighting an arduous legal battle.)

The librarian shook her head. "I'm sorry."

Chris' words were slow and calculated. "Can I change it? My book, can I write something new in there?"

The librarian's response was equally measured, carefully giving a right answer to the wrong questions. "The Library is by no means static—people are constantly writing and re-writing … But it's not so you can write whatever you want."

The group's eyes widened as the implications of this new wave of information crashed over them. Not only could they read about the future, they could affect it. Each of them formulating increasingly radical ideas of what this could mean, Lily began flitting her eyes across the bookshelves, searching hopefully for any volume that might bear her name on the spine. Lily dropped her eyes from the shelves to lock with the librarian's.

"Where's my book?"

2

FANTASY IS NOT NEAR SO MAGICAL AS REALITY

Having been intently questioned, the librarian stuck out the corner of her bottom lip and gave the mob what they wanted. She told them that everyone's books would be in the "people section" … After their discourse, and some amount of confused bickering, the party came to a unanimous decision that they all needed to find their own books. Our characters were all together in their other-worldly setting, with quite a proper motivation, being called to adventure; they had embarked on their journey, and the librarian reluctantly followed.

Chris confidently led the way, and as they walked, the librarian pointed to different books and sections with excitement, trying to pique the group's interest in the very magical Library. But they were intent on their mission, each for their own books.

"So," said Chris, "when we find our books, we can write anything we want in them, and it will come true?"

The librarian hesitated— "It will be your new truth. You'll be changing the reality of today, yesterday, and tomorrow; rewriting existence as you know it."

Chris nodded. "Good. Then I know what I was sent here for."

Sam replied, "Yeah, I know what I want."

Elizabeth, the mom, resolved, "I will make a better life for my kids."

"I dunno what you was brought here for," Jane remarked, "but I have things I'm gonna make right."

Jane went on to tell the group about her life as a popstar—supposedly well-known in the right circles, but her career was unjustly cut short. She was only able to release one album, which received little in the way of accolades because the system was designed to shunt real talent, and her criminal label refused to renew her contract. This was years and years ago, and of course, now her reputation was tarnished, and she could never find a deal anywhere else. Also, a few boyfriends along the way, none of whom really supported her like they ought to have, who tried to set her up with jobs like waitressing or something, as though that wouldn't be a cosmically offensive waste of talent.

Chris, now fed up with the long, contentious rant, and eager to change the subject, turned to address Sam.

"So, do you know what you're here for? What are you going to change?"

"Oh … well," Sam hesitated, and scratched the back of his neck, then without vim said, "I guess probably what I want most is true love, haha."

He finished with an awkward chuckle, thinking specifically of his best friend Beatrice, whom he had been desperately in love with for almost a decade.

"Hey now, atta boy, that's something, that's a goal!"

"Yeah …" Sam said, emboldened. "Girls are stupid. They don't like me, but they should. I'm a nice guy—"

Chris interrupted. "See, now I was cheated out of my inheritance. Some conspiracy cut me out of my uncle's will, and now my rotten cousin is squatting in a mansion that isn't his, and all of my siblings are living it up in their fancy cars, while I'm still here busting my chops for a paycheck. Well, I suppose my patience has paid off, because now I reckon I was brought here to fix it, to go back and put myself in the will. And I'm no malicious fellow; I'm reasonable enough. I'll divide it out fairly. I only want what's rightfully mine."

The librarian finally decided to cut in, "Listen, listen. You weren't brought here because you have any particular wrong to right in your life. You were brought here to see, to be shown, to learn something. You're in the Library of everything! Don't any of you want to try, I don't know, reading?"

"Hey now, you said we could change stuff, and I mean to!" said Chris. "Don't we have a right to make our lives what we want them to be? What they ought to be? We don't need to read about your raindrops or your tree leaves. We can spend all the time we want looking at those back home."

"Yeah, but you don't," muttered the librarian.

"Right now, I just want to get to my book. I have that right." Chris' last comment was met with rumbles of approval from the rest of the group. "Hey, so how big is this place anyways, how much farther have we got left?" he continued.

"The Library is a whole universe, I suppose in some ways it is as infinite as the worlds it describes."

"So, then, we could be walking forever?" Chris punctuated this sentence with a fling of his arm, sloshing his fishbowl.

"I should doubt so; books can only be so long," The librarian comforted them.

Lily took notice of Chris' fishbowl, and it suddenly struck her as a rather peculiar thing to carry around a Library, and the curiosity gave her enough courage to ask him about it.

"Hey, that's uh, that's an interesting fish—I've never seen a purple one like that. Where'd you get it?"

"I don't know. I was holding it when I got here, and I haven't had the heart to leave it."

"Pardon me, sir, perchance if I may just—"

These words were met with gasps, and pointed fingers, and at least one scream—as these words had come, with a polite English accent, from Barnacles, the fish.

"You can talk?!?" Chris leveled his eyes with the fish in awe.

18

"YoU cAn TaLK?—do you see how that question is redundant and rude? Of course I can talk. We are talking now, are we not?"

"But-but-but. Golly gee, my fish is talking to me," Chris stammered.

"Excuse me, Mister Chris, but, '*your* fish?' Are you *my* human? Or are we adults, above such silly chauvinism? And I'm not an it. My name is Barnacles, thank you."

After a brief silence, Lily chimed in. "Woah. A talking purple fish named Barnacles. Either I'm dreaming, or this is really a very magical place."

Barnacles rebuked her. "Is this world any more magical than yours? Which is stranger—a purple goldfish or a golden one?"

Chris looked down at the fish in his arms in astonishment.

"You know," Barnacles continued, "Schrödinger wrote 'This whole world is something we encounter only once … and we are astonished by what we find … yet are unable to say what we should have to have found in order not to be surprised.' So you say a talking fish is magic; is a talking primate not?"

Lily thought about this. Barnacles had a point.

Our protagonists made their way through the halls of the Library for hours—miles of bookshelves. At every new section the librarian would "eek" and "aww" and run her hand along the books, taking down any that struck her interest especially, such as the rather brief books that recounted the life span of a particular bolt of lightning, or the books that on the cover seemed like they might be most plain—such as the tale of a plastic spoon which after leaving the factory waited patiently in a box for three years before its brief moment of glory delivering blueberry yogurt to the fat face of a happy baby. Some of the neighboring spoons from the very box had quite a different fate, becoming vessels for cold pea-soup over a bickering divorced couple. The librarian loved to read and wanted to share the wonders of the Library with the guests. Her eyes grew wide as she read about a particular Atlantic Trench.

"Guys, there are sea monsters you wouldn't believe. I don't know why everyone is so obsessed with finding aliens—we haven't even found most of the things that live in the oceans! And just wait 'til we start digging for bones in the seabed … You don't even know!"

The whole trip was like this. The librarian would exclaim over many books in each section, but despite her enthusiasm, the party was uninterested. They were intent on getting to their own books while there was still time. Lily likewise wanted to get to her book (as she liked the thought of simply erasing all her flaws), but she was curious about the books, and sympathized with the librarian, so would listen to her and look at what she was showing.

"… and this jellyfish has rainbow disco strobe lights, like a freaking carnival sign!"

"Hey, librarian …" Lily was curious. "This Library has got to be, like, infinite—do you think it's real? Do all the books exist even if no one reads them?"

"In a way—yes and no. No, of course, because we're in a book right now, with a very finite number of pages. But, when we look at a book and see something—it's already something that has, to us, always been there and will always be there."

"What do you mean?"

"Well, is there a fire?"

"What do you mean?"

"Is there a fire?"

"Like right now, a literal fire? No, I guess."

"Ah, so even though you've seen fire a thousand times, there's millions of them burning around the world at any given moment—yet because you are not experiencing one right now, you say there is no fire."

"Well, okay, obviously fire exists, I meant, not right here right now."

"Of course it exists. Everything exists, everywhere, all the time. But your reality, your existence, is only the here and now. You're so bound by space and time that if you aren't actively watching a fire dance, feeling its warmth, hearing the roar and crackle—then it is only a figment of your mind. Either in memory, or in anticipation of the future. So, do these books all really exist? Of course, just not to you, or me, or anyone here."

"Really makes you feel small …" Lily said softly and sadly.

"You say it like you think it's a curse, not a blessing."

Lily chewed on this while the librarian gawked at more books.

"Do you have favorite books? Do you have your own collection?"

"No! We never take a book with us. The books are to be read in the moment, and then returned. Did everyone hear that? We do not take books!" The librarian shouted this again to everyone.

Lily questioned no further; the librarian had said it with a matter-of-fact sternness, and they all nodded with the wide awkward eyes of a non-thief charged with theft. They trekked on.

Walking alongside the librarian, taking up the rear of the pack, Lily thought. Sometimes thoughts feel more like something happening to us and less like something we're actively choosing to do. She spent much of her life thinking—she thought about herself, and what she needed to do, or not do, and how she looked, or didn't look, and what she wanted, or didn't want. Presently, she thought about what her story would be like and what she would change about it.

Riches were never considered, nor was royalty, fame, marriage … Lily knew what she most deeply wanted to change in her story. She considered the people she envied. They weren't necessarily the wealthiest, or the most popular—though sometimes they were. But the people she envied were never envied by her for those things. She envied them because of … well, them. They were happier than her, better than her, smarter than her, prettier than her, healthier than her. People with cooler personalities, better talent, better passions. People that didn't procrastinate, people with courage to do things she never could. Most importantly, people that made better decisions than she had. As Lily considered her book, and what changes she should make—she didn't feel the need to change her circumstances much at all. She wanted to change herself.

Like a role-playing video game where you can create your character, Lily found herself to be not at all the person she would make. She found nothing about herself to be particularly lovely. And not just physically—she didn't have the mind she should like, or the heart she should like either, for that matter. She wanted a perfect body, and she wanted a perfect soul. She knew what she would change about her book. Her mind had been made up, her idea had been solidified, and she thought to consult the librarian while they had some semblance of privacy trailing the rest of the group.

"You know," she started softly, "I don't think I'll do anything like the others. I don't want to be rich or famous or whatever. I just wish I was a better person. I'd go back and change myself from birth. Make myself wiser, and braver, and more caring, and more hardworking, and maybe prettier too, I guess."

Lily said the bit about prettier half-heartedly, as she was afraid of being seen by the librarian as shallow. The librarian turned towards Lily with a sparkle in her eye, and said with love, "How do you mean to go about making those changes in your book?"

"Well, I think I'd just write something like 'Lily is smart and kind and brave and passionate and …' yeah … like that?"

"I'm afraid that isn't quite how narrative works, dear. These books only contain truth, yes? So you can't write a story that says 'Lily is brave' but then have the rest of your story be full of you being … not brave. Does that make sense?"

"Oh. I think so. I can change everything then. How long will that take? I'll just go through and make all of my decisions … all of my actions … I'll rewrite my dialogues to be better. Yeah."

The librarian's words gushed warmth. "Honey, rewrite them how? Writing something like courage in one of these books takes … It takes knowing courage."

"I know what courage is. I know what discipline and smart is. I'm just not very good at doing it, I guess."

"Lily. I understand your desire to change some of the decisions you've made—but I think that every choice has consequences you don't quite understand. Even your failures make you better, if you let them. And if you want to change the habits of character you exercise in everyday life—well then, honey, change them! You don't need cosmic copy-editing abilities to start being a better character. And, when it comes to the way you are—your mind and body and soul, these things are unique, only you have them. It's what makes a Lily, and I really believe that this story needs a Lily. It needs you."

The librarian leaned over and squeezed Lily in an awkward walking side-hug and patted her shoulder.

"I think she'll figure it out," the librarian said wishfully about Lily, walking beside Elizabeth alone now as the two women watched the younger girl march ahead with her head down and arms folded.

"Hopefully sooner rather than later," Elizabeth answered.

"You remember what it was like to be her age. It's a lot," the librarian said, turning to Elizabeth.

Elizabeth kept looking straight. "I didn't really get to be a kid. I'm just here to make sure that my children get what I never got."

"How old are your kids?" The librarian sounded very invested.

"Ten is my oldest, and seven and two are my two boys."

"Children are so precious. I know you just want the best for them."

Elizabeth nodded. "It's hard. Life doesn't usually give many breaks, in my experience. Will changing my book really work?".

"You can change anything you want," said the librarian, "but the Library is so much more than that."

"What could be more important than taking care of my kids?" Elizabeth glared.

"You do take care of them, Elizabeth, I know you do. You have everything you need to be a mom. You've been doing it for ten years! People think of this Library as a way to get what they want, and they do get what they want, but—"

Elizabeth snorted. "Wow, I'm surprised that people like your regular Lady Gaga over here mess things up. Are most of your visitors as dumb as that?"

The librarian rolled her eyes. "Everyone that comes here thinks they have it all figured out."

"I don't have it all figured out." Elizabeth looked down for a moment, and then back up. "I just know my kids deserve better than what they're getting."

"They're lucky to have you as their mother."

The librarian didn't have anything else to say. Or, rather, Elizabeth didn't have anything else to hear. They kept walking, until they were confronted by something in the library …

3

DO NOT TRY
TO TAKE IT WITH YOU

THE QUIET OF THE LIBRARY was broken by shuffling somewhere in the shelves. Scurrying noises like a rat in the walls of a house. Everyone stopped.

"Uh-oh," said the librarian.

Then they saw it. Or saw … her? A lumpy, green, distorted, moss-ball of an old lady. She waddled around on bare, grey, veiny feet with long yellow toenails—her hands made a well-matching set. She pushed a shopping cart full of books, and pulled more off the shelves as though she were in Walmart. The librarian sighed.

"Guys, meet Spoon. This is what happens when you try to hold on to books."

Spoon sputtered and grumbled incoherently as she continued to raid the bookshelves. She had spite for the librarian's comment—but not so much as to stop her book-shopping.

"Still at it, huh Spoon? You couldn't even read one of those books, let alone all of them. Could you tell me about any of those books? Do you even read them anymore?" the librarian called out to the creature.

Spoon turned and opened her witch lips, and with a hateful, croaky, senile voice said, "Mines. Yous can't haves it. There'sis plentys books, these ones are Mines. Leave Spoon alones!"

"But, Spoon … can't you see it's destroying you? You need to go home."

"THIS IS MY HOMES!" the hag spat.

"No, Spoon. You were never meant to stay here. This place is only meant to show you something—to test your character, to teach and grow you, to take you from one place to another."

"I told yous. I told yous, silly librarians. I stays here. Yous go homes. I stays here!"

"Spoon, this place is … it's more like a dream. It will go away soon. You literally can't stay here."

"I don't leaves. I don't leaves. My books." Spoon's lucidity was slipping.

"Spoon, you love the books so much. I love them too—they're so beautiful and incredible. I love reading every one I get my hands on. But do you know what's better than books?"

"Huh?" Spoon perked.

"The reality that the books are written about. These books are just stories; they're not ultimate; they're not real. But they tell us about things that are real. Wouldn't you like that? I know that the book about an octopus is magnificent—but I can take you to a place where you could actually see and touch a real octopus! And no amount of mere words can replace that."

"Scary. Not reals. Can reads books. Can't reads a octsipusp."

"I know it's hard to imagine something better than the books. Do you remember when I told you about the people that lived in Plato's cave and only ever saw shadows? It would be hard to imagine the real things that cast those shadows, and hard to believe that colours and three dimensions exist. And I know that, compared to shadows, real things might seem terrifying. And the shadows become comforting and preferable. But please, look, it's destroying you. Trust me, and let the Library go."

Spoon looked up with sadness in her eyes. She was quiet for a moment. The librarian could see that, for a brief instant, Spoon understood. But the prospect of actually letting the books go was too much for her. She brought back her twisted scowl in response to the librarian's pity and returned to tending her cart.

The librarian's shoulders dropped, and she let out a sad sigh. She understood exactly what Spoon felt. She too was lured by the Library. She too was afraid of going home.

"But why? What does she want with them?" Chris asked.

"Just to have them, I guess. But especially for no one else to have them. Go on, I dare you to try to read a book out of her cart."

Chris had no intention of the sort. Soon enough, Spoon had slapped her nasty feet around the corner out of the hallway, muttering absurdities and growing her book-pile as she went. The librarian would explain this to the group—as was her job.

"See, Spoon was a part of a visiting group a long time ago, just like you guys. But when it was time, she wouldn't let the books go so she could leave. So, she's stuck here now, hoarding books, unable to even really read them anymore. It's quite sad. I love this Library, but she was obsessed with it. She replaced adventure, relationships, and real life with a fantasy. It's like loving a portrait of your husband instead of your actual husband. And she didn't just confuse it for the real world—she preferred it to the real world. She tried to make it be something it can never be—something ultimate and final, her purpose, her joy. But it's just, it's a shadow, a symbol, a sketch, an allegory."

The group sat in a long, awkward silence, now aware of real consequences to this place. Lily thought to ask the librarian, "Hey, how did you get here? Are you stuck here forever too?"

"Haha, no. I was a part of the last group that came here. I was asked to stay to help guide the next one—I'll go home soon, too."

"I don't know about all that business with that Spoon character," said Chris.

"A proper muppet indeed." Barnacles the fish harrumphed his agreement.

"I sure don't want to end up like that …" mumbled Sam.

"I ain't gonna end up like that. But I know I'm staying here till I get my story straight," said Jane.

4

THE GOOD AUTHOR

T HE LIBRARIAN'S ATTEMPTS to get the others to
pick up a book were further thwarted, as now
everyone shared an unspoken fear of somehow having
their minds poisoned like Spoon's. Chris was content
enough to watch the librarian; a peculiar character she was.
Every now and again, the librarian would jot down a little
note in one of the books before returning it to its shelf.

"What are you writing?" Chris inquired.

The librarian, smiling to have been asked, said, "Oh
just little things that I see, I guess. Sometimes I plant a
flower or something. Or, here, look at this—" she said,
handing over a book titled *Serenity the Sea Turtle*.

Chris read what the librarian presented. Reading
a book that someone else was holding while both were

walking proved to be too difficult, and so Chris shuffled Barnacle's fishbowl to his offhand so that he could hold on to the book.

Chris' experience reading was as strange as his experience of finding himself in the Library. He felt as though he was really there; he couldn't quite say that he could actually see and smell and hear the scene, but he could certainly have said that he felt what the scene felt like.

"It's a baby sea turtle."

"That's right. And what's the conflict?"

"It needs to make it to the ocean, but it can't. Seagulls are attacking it."

Chris gasped as he read the end of this poor baby sea-turtle, torn apart by talons and bills. It made him want to cry, until the librarian consoled him, leaned over, and scribbled down a new ending, the simplest little change of giving the turtle a small bit of foliage to hide under. And *voilà*, the turtle made it to the ocean—to safety.

"That's wonderful," Chris said admiringly, feeling much better.

"Well, now if you read on, it gets eaten by a tiger shark or something. Everything has to die at some point in this story. All I did was ever so slightly change when and how."

"So then why did you help the turtle? What's the point in tampering at all?"

"Because it all has a purpose, it isn't chaotic and random like it might seem, there's a bigger picture, and this is the tiny part of that picture that's in front of me, here and now. I can make something a little better, like my own little miniature work of art within the greater piece, if you will. I'm not just put here to be a passive observer to the story, I'm an actor in this play, too. I have my own part to move the narrative forward. Everyone has the chance to add to the story, for better, or, for worse."

Chris now was less sure of the goodness of the librarian's deed. Was getting eaten by a seagull in youth objectively worse than getting eaten by a shark in adulthood? In many ways, it seemed potentially preferable. The librarian added insight—

"The real kicker is that now, there's a book out there for some poor seagull that goes hungry. Maybe it means the difference between starving to death or surviving another season. And if you were reading the seagull's book, you probably couldn't help but cheer for the bird."

"So, are you saying there's no such thing as good and bad? It's all relative?"

"You ask good questions, Chris. I like that," the librarian said cheerfully. "It's true that every sunrise is someone else's sunset. But the sadness of starvation doesn't negate the sadness of getting eaten … Chris, do you think a painting has value? Say, a painting of a great wave?"

"Of course it does."

"Does a real wave have value, like a tsunami? Someone painted that, too. Have you ever really looked at a real wave? It's so much more beautiful than any human imitation of it could ever be. Does a tsunami have value?"

"No. A painting doesn't hurt anyone. The destruction of houses, the loss of life, that's evil, that makes a tsunami evil!"

The librarian answered calmly, "You're right. A piece of art doesn't do much good if everyone is too dead to enjoy it. The tsunami isn't a go-go dancer—it doesn't exist just for everyone to gawk at. It serves a narrative purpose. Just like seagulls and turtles serve a purpose."

"What purpose could a tsunami have? Maybe if natural disasters only killed bad people, I could see that. But they don't. We're all just poor baby turtles waiting to get eaten sooner or later."

"No, honey, don't you see? It's a story, we're all characters. Literally, someone wrote us into being, prepared for us a script, and cast us into these roles; don't you see?"

"Yeah, well, the author of my book must be some sick sadist."

"Then the author of all books must be some sick sadist. You're not gonna hurt his feelings by hurling those insults. Try instead to think of the narrative."

"What do you mean?"

"What's a story that you like?"

"Ummmm … *Star Wars*?"

"George Lucas wrote that, is he evil?"

"What?"

"Why did Darth Vader exist?"

"What do you mean? Because George Lucas wrote him in the script."

"Well, that's true, and reason enough, I suppose. But why? He was pretty evil—choking people to death with the Force, cutting off Luke Skywalker's hand with a lightsaber, (sorry for the spoiler), blowing up entire planets with the Death Star …"

"Because that story needed a bad guy … But real life doesn't need a bad guy. I know I certainly don't need a bad guy! There could be no Darth Vader, no Death Star, no seagulls, no tsunamis, no back-stabbing family!"

"There … could be. But … Which is happier to you—the beginning of *Star Wars*, or the end? Luke Skywalker could have just stayed home and skipped the whole adventure, roll credits—If we're going that far—the baby turtle could have just never been hatched at all."

"Yeah, but that's still just a story. Those characters aren't real; they don't feel real suffering like we do …"

The librarian laughed at the irony of Chris' comment. "All characters are real, inasmuch as they are reflections of their author. And I'd argue that if some characters aren't quite so solid as you and me, it is because their author isn't quite so solid as ours. But perhaps that's beside the point for you, so instead I'll ask—which stories have the happiest endings?"

"Umm, I don't know. The ones where the bad guys lose, and the good guys win?"

"No, that's stupid, sorry. The stories with the happiest endings are the stories that have the most conflict. The best characters are the ones that are really tested. And I'm not just talking about novels and scripts. Think of some of the coolest people you know, people that you can really talk to about anything—they're the people that have really been through it, huh, and people that have something to be proud of are people that had to earn it."

Understanding dawned on Chris. The librarian continued.

"There would be no such thing as courage without a thing such as fear. There would be no unconditional love unless there existed possible conditions; no faith that could conquer mountains unless there were mountains to be conquered. No such thing as generosity without disparity. No satisfaction without thirst. Victory without a battle is really no victory at all … Painters use shadows to make the highlights shine all the brighter. And for you to launch your complaints and insults is just as silly as Skywalker complaining that George Lucas made Darth Vader too big and scary. In the end, a softer villain would have made for a weaker hero, which would have made for a poorer story. Do you see?"

"So what? The turtle dies so that it can have tension? Don't you think, if given the choice, the turtle would prefer to be boring and uneaten?"

"The character dies in that story, sure, everyone does. But the character, the heart of them, lives on. Characters that have died and characters that haven't yet are both equally real, they just occupy different time slots. These words on a page have been recorded forever. Someone could write a book about a trillion years filled with nothing, but someone who lives a short while and has a story to tell will fill a book. Years are cheap; pages, instead, are our currency. Plot, theme, character development and arcs, moral, sentiment, narrative … Both books exist outside of time, in this instant, but one is so much bigger than the other."

Becoming aggravated, Chris took a moment to prepare his rebuttal. "Tell me, librarian, where is the big picture? What is the point? How about emperor Nero, or Unit 731? Where's the narrative in that?! You think you could look into the eyes of someone who's been through hell and tell them that it was all part of the script?"

The librarian swallowed. "… When I first got here, I was overcome with a curiosity about how the Library came to be, who wrote it, and who was to blame for my, my … suffering. Who would write any of this?!" Gesturing around to the bookshelves around her, "with worms that burrow into the eyes of children to blind them, mosquitoes which carry diseases to kill so many … tsunamis that destroy cities, and all the evil that people commit every day. I was so angry about it all. It was clear to me that every story, every character, has an author and what a horrible author I must have …"

The librarian couldn't help but tear up.

"And then I met him. And he talked to me. He showed me. Not the whole narrative; I can't read or understand the whole narrative. But he showed that there is a narrative, and that he really does care. He told me about how he sits there and carefully writes me, and prepares things for me, and sometimes it's really hard, and I don't understand it all, but I know that it all has a reason."

"So then what did you edit about your book; when you first came here?"

"I didn't."

"What do you mean? There was nothing you wanted to fix or change? Everything was perfect for you?"

"No, of course my life wasn't, and still isn't perfect. I'll be going back to it soon. There are a lot of things that are … hard. And things I don't understand. When I got here, all I wanted was to make it so I could have kids. I just wanted to be a mom …"

A solemn silence enveloped the two.

"Look, the author, like, he … he makes each of us unique, and gives us our own trials and difficulties to develop us. Like any good author should. I used to be so sure that if I just had that one thing then I would be happy, that it would be okay. But it isn't so. Sometimes he's made characters like that, you know, characters that are content enough to just do what they want—one-dimensional things, with no real conflict or meaningful growth … Happy people are never people who have nothing to be sad about. And as much as it hurts, I'm so glad that he cares enough to spare me from that. So, yes, he cuts. But he doesn't cut with a criminal's switchblade, he cuts with a surgeon's scalpel."

"What do you mean? How is the author not evil? That is a curse! That isn't right, it isn't fair. You have every reason to be angry! A baby would make you happy, and I'm sure you'd make a great mom."

"No, Chris. What isn't fair is existence; all the absurd blessings; the ridiculous care and detail that has been put into me and my life. Do you have any idea how absolutely nuts childbirth is? It's unbelievable, it's obscene, and it seems reckless that it should happen to anybody at all. I don't have the right to demand a baby any more than a flower has the right to demand that water should fall from the sky—"

"Okay, but it's still cruel. It still is a cruel thing to deny you that happiness."

"Because I'm the best agent for my own happiness? Chris, I'm the number one enemy to my own happiness. And you're the number one enemy of yours. Who has lied to you most in your life? Who has sabotaged greater? Disappointed most? Who has robbed you of more joy than yourself? If there's one person that you cannot trust with your own happiness—it is you."

"Don't feed me that! You don't believe that! You know you'd be happy if you were a mom."

Chris was right. The librarian still wanted very badly to be a mother and have children of her own.

"Of course I would be happy. But listen, I'm telling you, the reason that I can't is so that I can be the character that I am. So that we can have the conversation that we're having. And maybe so someone who reads this in the future can receive hope. Eh, but what do I know?"

Christopher marched ahead and huffed about how he'd make himself happy if only he were allowed to, if only other people were out of the way. The librarian sighed.

5

SIX DEGREES
OF SEPARATION

THE GROUP BECAME increasingly restless as they made no discernible progress toward their books.

Chris spoke up. "Hey, how long do we have? To change our books?"

The librarian rolled her eyes. "I can't tell you that."

"You don't know? Or you ain't gon' tell us?" clapped Jane.

"Yes," the librarian answered decisively.

Barnacles the fish had been developing a thought for some time. "Ma'am, it would seem as though you've indeed read our books before. Would you not know, then, precisely their location?"

"Well … the Library is infinite, and to find any specific book or section within you have to use the Library Catalogue."

"The what?" Sam asked.

"Here, look!" The librarian pulled a book at random off the nearest shelf and opened the very back cover, revealing an appendix full of intra-Library cross-references.

"Like the Dewey Decimal System?" asked Lily.

"Yes, Lily, kind of like that. Every book has a sort of glossary linking all the books it references. Look, here's an example."

The specific book the librarian had grabbed was about an ancient silver shekel, circulated for hundreds of years, part of that coin's story was the many long years it spent in a leather purse—the leather of which came from a certain Mesopotamian goat named Evie. That goat's book was referenced in the shekel's book.

"See, here it is!" The librarian ran along some shelves and fingered through some books until she was able to find the book about Evie the goat.

Barnacles was a smart fish, and he pieced together the librarian's plan rather quickly. "We ought to then find a book that in some way has to do with ourselves."

"Well …" the librarian continued, "your books are in the people section. Books aren't organized alphabetically or anything like that, they are organized based on narrative connectedness—and nothing is more connected to people than other people. To get your books, we have to get to the people section—it should be cake from there … the only thing is that, to get to the people section in an infinite Library would take an infinite amount of time … So you guys will have to find a very specific book."

"What book?" Chris interrupted impatiently.

"A book about the Library itself."

"And how come you don't have this book? Where is it?" Chris screamed.

"I don't know where it is, I'm telling you how to find it."

"And you're just telling us this now!?! You said we wouldn't be walking around forever, you said you knew where we were going!"

"I never pretended to know where we are going, and you guys never bothered to ask for directions. I've been following you, remember?"

Chris hoed and hummed in embarrassment, "Well, how do we get this *Library of Everything* book?"

Barnacles was capable of basic pattern recognition, and so answered for Chris. "We ought to be able to find it in the appendix of any book, right, miss librarian?"

The librarian said, "The Library Catalogue, like the Library itself, is infinite. So you can't find any book in just any other book, that would be stacking turtles all the way down. What there certainly is, however, is a book about our adventure, the lot of us in the Library of Everything here and now. And how we'd have to find that book would be to find something we all have in common—we need a book that we're all in. We're all in this book."

Chris threw up his arms again. "And how in the blazes are we supposed to find that!?"

The librarian's eyes sparkled. "Have you ever heard of the principle of 'six degrees of separation'? The world is smaller than you think. I'm sure you can do it, like how this shekel is connected to this goat Evie—there's a person you've all met, or a chair you've all sat in … you all share narrative threads, you just have to find them!"

The group took some convincing, but the librarian insisted that it was a part of their journey, and so they began about it, each one wandering off in their own direction to find a book to which they had some connection.

Lily turned first to her right, and upon reading the titles of books about starfish, she doubted she should have much in common with those, as she had never been to the ocean. And so she walked across to the other side of her immediate library hallway, and instead pulled down a book about a beehive.

Lily thought to herself that bees were cute, and perhaps she had come into contact with a bee from this hive. It was certainly possible. So she read through, flipping pages and being quite astonished at the intricate inner-workings of beehives. She grew somewhat hopeful when she discovered that this colony of bees lived on the same continent as her, and on the same half of that continent, no less. However, she never did read about any interactions with any girl named Lily, until she started reading about all the various flowering plants which were pollinated by bees from this hive. And there was where she found a possible connection to herself in this book: A florist in her hometown sourced flowers from a garden pollinated by a bee from a colony whose queen descended from the hive Lily was reading about. She turned to the very back of the book and, after quite some searching, found *Fanatic Florals* in her hometown, referenced there in the book about this beehive.

Lily set off to find the book for the flower shop, which couldn't have been too far away from all these other books with heavy connections to 21st century East Coast America. And sure enough, it was only a couple dozen rows over—and, annoyingly, high enough for her to have to climb one of the Library's rolling ladders to reach. But there it was, *Fanatic Florals* written on the spine—what an interesting book it was. Lily read all about people from her hometown that she knew coming and going in and out of this small flower shop, making conversation. The books of the library were peculiar— she recognized people she knew even if she hadn't quite remembered their names, the way the book described them and presented their dialogue was as good a jog to memory as making eye contact with an old acquaintance, even if she couldn't place exactly where she knew them from, she recognized them nonetheless; reading, she felt the urge to lower her eyes as she would in person, but had to remind herself that book-people couldn't see her.

She read and read—scouring pages for anything that might possibly be linked to her, anyone that she remembered seeing with flowers … anything. And then it was there. A pretty little single lily stem picked and paid for and carried out the store by one Fredrick Dinkle, who had walked into Fanatic Florals on a September afternoon. Lily grimaced and rubbed her temples. She now had to walk a few shelves over and find the book for that particular lily stem, where she read about her old classmate Freddy, who was the dorkiest kid she had ever known—small, awkwardly proportioned, with inch-thick glasses, and clothes that were too big and yet somehow also too small.

She read from the perspective of the flower, which had been carefully and proudly selected by Freddy for a special purpose. All of Lily's cringey memories bubbled up against her. In Junior high Freddy had the biggest crush on Lily. The only person in her school who she felt paid much attention to her was the last person she wanted attention from. Not only did he not seem to care that Lily always sat alone in the corner, with her hat pulled down almost over her eyes and her hood up and her earbuds in—he seemed fascinated with it, like it was his personal mission to unravel her mysteries. Freddy was never horribly flirtatious or anything, just overly interested in her and friendly to her. Lily had always thought that she was nice enough to Freddy when he sat by her at lunch or walked up to her in the halls, but one day on her birthday …

Lily read about a flower that traveled home with this kid and slept upon his nightstand, eagerly awaiting its big day. The flower rode the bus to school and was finally presented with a kind "Happy birthday, Lily." What a proud moment for the flower—a new owner and a new home and a grand purpose. It had been a simple enough gesture. Lily awkwardly said thanks, and walked away. Until she imagined all the girls that would point and "ooh" and start rumors about her and Freddy sitting in a tree. Lily read about how this proud young flower had been abruptly shoved into the depths of Lily's backpack, sandwiched between old homework and an English Literature textbook.

Freddy's hurt expression now haunted Lily. But she could feel the eyes on her now as she had then. Except there had been no eyes on her. Reading through the perspective of the poor flower, she read about herself simply as one character in the greater tale that this flower had to tell. Nobody really cares that much about what nerds give flowers to other nerds, and even if they did, Lily realized that it was silly of her ever to care so much. She regretfully read on about that poor flower being smushed around in a dark backpack all day, and pulled out that night a sad, flat, trodden thing. Lily closed the book then.

"I found a book that I'm in," Lily said solemnly to the librarian, holding up the book about the lily. "What do I do now?"

"Oh, how delightful!" the librarian squealed with glee at the promising progress. "Now we just have to find a book referenced in that book that has all of us in it!"

And so, they all set about it. Sam was rather quickly able to find the book for a peanut that made it into a jar of peanut butter, which he sold to a customer at the general store he worked at. Jane insisted on finding the book for an album of hers. She didn't, but she did find a certain delivery truck that had once driven by whilst a song of hers played passingly somewhere. Elizabeth was able to find the book for an apartment complex she had lived in. It wasn't much trouble finding water that Barnacles had swum in. And after much searching, Chris found a book for a squirrel that had lived in a tree that used to be in his backyard.

The group had all sat around on the soft carpet of the library. Many of them had multiple books open in front of them and they were all searching for any reference to each other's books.

"Anyone found anything yet?" Sam asked restlessly as he looked around at the mess of books about them.

Chris didn't look up from his book. "We never will if you don't stop complaining like that!"

Elizabeth blinked slowly and turned to Sam. "When we do, we'll let you know, kiddo."

And then, as though someone had been shot, the librarian squealed. "It's here, it's here! Look look look!"

She pointed to Jane's book at the delivery truck, and one of the many parcels it had delivered—one of them had been to Christopher's mother. Chris and Jane had a connection. Next, Elizabeth soon found a distributor of decorative quartz pebbles that had been used in an aquarium Barnacles once swam in, and also a flower vase in her own apartment. Their progress was snowballing. As they found more and more connections, they could all feel themselves coming closer to their shared goal. Until it finally clicked.

Jane's delivery truck, and the letter of Chris' mother (which had been news of her brother's death), and Lily's flower, and Sam's peanut butter, and Barnacle's water, and pieces of Elizabeth's apartment, all had a commonality in that they each had at one time or another traveled a lone stretch of highway, from nowhere to nowhere in southwest Wyoming. Roads did connect the world, after all. A long stretch of lonely road that had carried little pieces of all their stories. US Highway 191. The group all scrambled at once, looking along all the bookshelves rapidly in an attempt to find the book.

Highway 191, Jane was the first to get to it, and she tore it open to the back, where the rest of the group huddled about, seeing each of themselves referenced in the appendix of this unassuming highway—each of their stories, and the focal point of the intersection of their lives was this story here, *The Library of Everything*. The reference number showed that it was close. Very close to them.

"It should be right here!" Chris declared, surveying the multitude of books in their immediate hall.

"I agree," the librarian said, double checking her references. "It should be."

And as they had this discussion, Lily caught out of the corner of her eye, motion within one of the bookshelf units very high up, just too tall for her to make out the titles on the spines.

"What's that?" Lily called the librarian's attention to the book that had moved. "It's moving."

"No …" the librarian said as she rolled the nearest ladder over and began to climb. Everyone turned their attention to the book in question.

As the librarian topped her ladder, the title of this book was right in her face: *The Library of Everything*.

"The girl's right. I swear I saw it move," Chris shouted upward.

But the librarian slowly studied the nearly imperceptible motion as this book very slowly created for itself more width between its neighbor books and whispered to herself, "he's writing." Then, yelling down to the rest, "It isn't moving, it's growing."

The librarian quickly snatched up *The Library of Everything* and scuttled down the ladder. "Now we just have to write in it that we can find the people section."

She opened it up to about page 52 and, with her pencil in hand, she prepared to add a bit about the lot of them finding their own books. Everyone crowded around her in anticipation.

As the librarian searched for the appropriate place to make such an edit—she said her lines as she read them, "Oh …" lowering her pencil now, "I think … we should just keep going a little further …" and she put *The Library of Everything* away on the shelf, without making a single edit.

6

THE WRONG KIND
OF APATHY

THE GROUP had been confused and apprehensive when the librarian put *The Library of Everything* away as she had made no edits at all. Chris demanded to know why she would put all their hard work to waste, and why the librarian wouldn't follow their plan through to the end to get them to their books. However, the librarian was in a state of awe and insisted that they only needed to go a little further. And it was not long before the section for people became visible to them.

"There it is!" Jane shouted triumphantly.

"Finally," sighed Chris.

This section was unlike the others; up until now, the books had been rather uniform in their appearance, but in the people section, every book was unique. Lily received an answer from the librarian before she could ask the question.

"Welcome to the people section. Every book represents a human life. You can tell a lot about a person by looking at the cover of their book. The size and shape and design of the book come from the personality of the main character. Note that the length of the book does not indicate how long someone lived—there are plenty of die-youngers that have one heck of a story to tell. And there are plenty of people that lived a hundred-plus years with next to nothing to show for it."

Every spine was labelled. Every soul that ever was, is, or would be … Theodore, Michael, Harper, Kænhetda, Brook, Gage, Apricity, Johnny, Queen Elizabeth II, Selah, Robert, Nameless, Olive, etc. Many booklets, pamphlets almost, of babies, characters that never got to live much of a story. Many of the books had never been assigned written names, and too many of the books were titled *Emma*. Please stop naming your kids Emma. There were magicians and monsters, gurus and hobos, tribal hunter-gatherers and astronauts …

"How are we supposed to find our books in all of this?" the group grumbled.

The librarian, in her typical mystical fashion—"You often can only find what you're looking for when you stop looking for it. If all you focus on is yourself, you'll lose yourself. If you want to find yourself, you have to take your eyes off of yourself. Turn your gaze outwards."

The librarian reached up to one of the shelves and pulled down a book at random. It was a one-inch-thick glossy blue paperback, reminiscent of some government training manual. It smelled like glue. The name on the spine was Evan.

"See, look at this guy. He was born in Massachusetts in 1992. Evan. He was the youngest sibling and always had to fend for himself. He wanted to be a musician, but he fell in love, and family got in the way. He was shipped off to the Gulf War, and while he was away, his baby daughter died of flu and his wife left. He lost everything. He was a hard and bitter soldier, given to drink. When he got back, he became a hitman for east coast gangs … Killing debtors isn't so different from killing enemy combatants. Look—"

The librarian was cut off by several simultaneous interruptions. Nobody wanted to hear Evan's sob story—they all were eager to find their own books. The librarian sighed.

"Yeah, you guys can do whatever you want. Your own books are somewhere here among the billions. Good luck, I guess. But … please be careful."

The gang split up and began racing around the bookshelves, looking for the book they came here for. The organization was peculiar—people were sorted in part by location, in part by date, and in part by personality. The whole section was a complex network of shelves and books arranged such that each story tied into the ones around it—thousands of little narrative webs, insignificant encounters, lifelong romances, accidents that changed lives …

Before they got too far, the librarian stopped Lily by holding her shoulder. "Lily, wait."

The others hurried ahead as Lily and the librarian lagged behind. "What is it?"

"Shh, listen."

Everyone else heard it also, as they ventured deeper into the Library halls—the muttering, cursing, wailing. Tormented souls.

Chris, who was some hundred paces ahead, stopped, turned back, and stated the obvious, "We're not alone in here."

The librarian shook her head and didn't raise her voice, but she didn't have to for Chris and the rest to understand that there were others.

Chris and Sam rounded a library shelf to observe an old, skinny, wispy-haired man, with a book in his arms and a pen in hand, pacing back and forth. Mumbling obscenities to himself, scratching angrily at the book, completely absorbed in his writing, he made no acknowledgment of Chris.

"Who is that? What is he doing?" Sam whispered to Chris.

Barnacles answered first, "I should suspect that fellow is doing what we mean to do. He's changing his book."

Chris suspected the same, and so called out to the old fellow, "Good day, sir! Me and my friends just arrived. Is that your own book? You really found it?"

The old man looked up for a moment and squinted for a moment. And then spoke way too loudly, (as old people often do). "Oh. Yep, very well, thank you."

"How is it going for you?" Chris pressed for more information.

The old man had looked back to his book. "Yep. Of course. Mhm."

Sam and Chris and Barnacles all looked at one another and shrugged (which was quite the feat for Barnacles, who had no shoulders). Chris put his hand up as a barrier of secrecy and spoke low, "He's obviously a bit senile; we ought to leave him alone." The rest agreed, and they moved on.

Some ways away, but not so very far off, Jane stood fixed in the Library; she had found another source of the sounds that haunted this part of the Library. Lily and the librarian approached her and saw what she had been looking at—a little girl, maybe only fourteen. She stood over a book that lay open on the floor of the Library, red faced, fists clenched over a pen, and crying a terrible cry.

They approached her pitifully and awkwardly, (if there is a good approach to a crying stranger, I've yet to find it), and the librarian set her hand on the girl's back and spoke first. "There there, honey, it's okay. Let's get you home."

The girl immediately threw off the librarian's hand, turned and screamed, "NO! I have to fix it! Get away from me!" And then resumed her sobbing.

The group backed up to give the girl her space. Jane called the girl a brat under her breath.

Lily asked, "Is that … her book?"

The librarian nodded. "She came here in my group; her name is Brenda. She found her book and … well … it isn't what she wanted it to be."

Jane said, "So why don't she just fix it?"

The librarian answered, "It looks like she's trying. But I guess she isn't the biggest fan of the stuff she writes."

They left the girl there crying, and also the man there muttering. As they eagerly searched the halls, they encountered many others who had already found their books. Elizabeth tried consoling one, Chris asked another for directions, but they each were absorbed in their own books. Some were crying, others were quite angry or even violent, all were completely lost in their own work. This cast a shadow of fear over the group, who feared their books might be as painful to read. However, it didn't matter how bad things might be, because they were on their missions to fix it.

Jane was the first to stop, in front of a particular volume, yelling, "THERE YOU ARE!"

7

PENNING DESTINY

JANE

J ANE'S BOOK WORE several coats of tacky, neon-coloured paint vandalistically smeared over the patinaed leather cover underneath. The layers of paint were peeling on the spine to reveal her name written on it with love. Jane held the large book without ceremony and spent almost no time reading it. She had work to do. Producing a pen from her purse, she began furiously scribbling in her book, mumbling to herself.

"There. I never shoulda lost that record deal—and now I didn't."

She flipped back in her book to check the results, and a nasty grin grew on her face. Her singing career had taken off. She was rich and famous and fairly successful until …

"No, that ain't right. What? Why would I do that?"

Jane's brow furrowed as she scanned through her story. She found that shortly after her career took off, so did her stability. She still felt like a failure, washed up, and sad. She wrapped her Lamborghini around a pole, spent time in jail, and stopped being able to perform …

"That doesn't make sense. Why would I quit music? I'm HOMELESS?!? Well, I can fix that … Top singer in the USA? Don't mind if I do. Guess who's platinum now … I knew I was always meant for something big."

When she was done tweaking the details of her story to her wildest dreams and every whim, she paged forward to see her future. But she didn't have one. Only six years after winning her Grammy, Jane would overdose on heroin and die, feeling worthless and alone.

Jane gripped her pen tighter. For hours she paced and edited and rewrote. And no matter what success she gave herself, her end was always equally as sad. Even when she found the right combination of childhood experiences and adult therapy to keep her clean from drugs and STDs—her fame lost its luster quickly when she didn't capitalize on enjoying it, and her story would still find a way to end up in misery. Tears of frustration carried mascara to paint black stripes on her cheeks. She was defeated, but still she worked at it.

SAM

"Okay, Sam, you can do this. If I were my book, where would I be?"

Sam knew his book the moment he spotted it. He could feel that it was his; it was just like his journal that he had at home under his bed. The journal he had at home was full of angsty poems and hopelessly romantic sentiments. But this book was full of genuine stories. Sam's breath quickened and his heart palpated as his mind raced. He would be able to visit one of his most frequented memories—himself and the girl of his dreams, Beatrice, first falling in love.

They had practically grown up together, having met freshman year of high school and hitting it off immediately clicking as close friends. Bea had a boyfriend when they met, so at first their relationship was platonic. But the moment he knew he was in love with her was just several weeks into their relationship—when Bea's boyfriend callously dumped her and broke her poor heart. She tapped on Sam's window that night, having walked all the way to his house through rain. Her wet hair framed her big, green, gemstone eyes, running with tears and raindrops. As soon as he let her in, she buried her face into his neck, thanking him for being there, as he asked what was wrong.

Reading this now, Sam could feel how he felt then. The memory was so visceral, the cool wetness of her clothes, her shivers, and the goosebumps on her arms around him. What Sam hadn't remembered so well, until he read it from his book, was the specifics of their conversation—or rather, how Bea had mostly just vented about Johnny, her recent ex. Sam comforted her as she cried, assuring her that not all guys were like that, promising her that one day she'd find a man that would treat her how she deserved to be treated; silently promising to be that man.

He'd been in love with Bea since that night years ago. He'd never been able to tell her how he felt. Being in the friend-zone sucked. Sam would fix things.

"She keeps me at arm's length and goes around and dates all these jerks that break her heart and then comes crying to me. She doesn't know what she's doing."

Sam fumed about how the whole thing was all one big game of mating displays and flirting. Waiting the right amount of time before texting back, acting dismissive, being impressive and unimpressed, being mysterious, and making it clear that you had plenty of other romantic options. Sam understood the principles well; he had even read a book or two on the art of attraction. But it was too late for that; he had forever ruined his first impression with her by being her dorky, emotional friend in high school. Bea liked having him as a friend too much to ever risk having him as more. And so, Beatrice was swept away by every guy that was better than him at playing the game. And, it seemed, the worse they treated her, the more obsessed with earning their approval she would be. There was an inverse correlation between a guy's pickup skills and his abilities as an actual loving boyfriend. Somehow, Bea never saw what was so plain.

The thought crossed his mind to find and read Beatrice's book and see what or how she really thought of him; he knew she was in love with him. They'd always been in love. But soon it wouldn't matter what was in her book, because he'd put them together. It wasn't right that they weren't already together.

"Ugh. Girls ..." Sam muttered, reading through all the painful memories.

And so he did it. He went back and twiddled the little details. He made himself perfect at it, at least so far as he knew how from the books. He reached back into the events of his history and tweaked it all. Conversations with Bea were now laced with false coolness; he undid all the dorky and desperate things—calling late at night, writing cringy poems, smothering her.

But in doing this, he watched as their whole relationship and his whole story was altered. She had never come to him that night after her breakup. He had lost his very most treasured memory. He was losing her. It wasn't enough to just be more charming, he needed fate on his side.

And so he didn't only alter his behaviours to line up with his pickup artistry skills, he also played with chance. He had read somewhere that any two people can fall in love given the right circumstances, so certainly he needed only to give Bea, his soulmate, the right circumstances to fall in love with him. He put himself with her as lab partners, ran into her in the hall, put her on the same shift at work, gave her a flat tire on the highway just in time for him to come save her, and even got her stuck at his place in a snowstorm once.

And it worked. He was shaking with excitement as he read about their first hookup in that snowstorm— even better than the night in the rain he had foregone, as now himself, and not her ex-boyfriend Johnny, was the sole object of her attention and affection in that moment. He wanted to go back home right now and kiss her for real. But, he knew how fragile this was, and he knew that this Library was a once in a lifetime opportunity. He had to secure this thing. So, he scrolled forward to make sure that nothing catastrophic came in between him and Beatrice living happily ever after, and it was a good thing that he did. Because, sure enough, their relationship only lasted a couple months. She broke his heart and left him to go back to her jerk ex, Johnny.

"Why? We were so happy together; I don't get it. I didn't do anything wrong!"

Sam went to re-touch things. Perhaps he had taken not being needy to the extreme, and he was too emotionally distant once they got together. He threw in a couple extra romantic gestures and wrote Johnny into a lethal motorcycle accident for good measure. And, at this point, Sam didn't even feel like reading around looking for where the wedding was; he was gonna write their marriage right here and now, before anything else could ruin their happily ever after.

And it was beautiful, the best day of Sam's life. He had everything he ever wanted, living the life of his dreams with his soulmate, Beatrice. He couldn't help but flip forward to get a glimpse of their future and children, but what he read cut him like a sword.

"… You … cheat on me? And divorce me, and … fight me for custody over our baby?"

Sam read out loud with a rock in his throat and tears rolling down his face. How could she do this? He sat and cried in his broken heart.

"This doesn't make sense. You were my soulmate … Why would you do this?"

"No, honey." The librarian walked up behind Sam. "She wasn't your soulmate. She's just kind of floundering around with men. You're not the first heart she's broken, and you won't be the last. Sam, you're seeing Beatrice through rose-coloured glasses, because you're in love with her, but she can never be what you want her to be. I know you want her so badly, but you're not going to find what you need in her."

"Then I'll fix her."

Sam cleared his throat, stood up, and wiped his tears. With his book in his arms, he took off down the halls of the Library with a purpose.

"Sam, don't, you can't. Please, let her go …" The librarian was ignored.

Sam stomped along the shelves, looking left and right for the book of his soulmate. He couldn't tell how long it took him to find it. Hours? But there it was, covered in pink sequins. He held the two books side by side, his and hers, and smiled at how perfect they were for each other. Opening up Bea's book, he knew exactly what he needed to do. Erase every boy that ever broke her heart, make it so that he was the only guy she'd ever be with. He needed to tweak her, so that she truly loved him, and would never leave him. And it was hard work; every change he made had its effects. Removing her heartbreak made her more secure and confident, and therefore less dependent on him. Then he had to go back to his book and readjust his whole strategy to winning her over. Back and forth Sam went, toiling over the two books.

When he had a result that somewhat resembled himself and Bea living "happily ever after," he wasn't himself, and Bea wasn't Bea. Not the one he knew and loved. He was infatuated with her for her rebelliousness, but he had taken that from her so that she might not rebel against him. He obsessed over her for her wildness, but he had tamed her so that he could keep her. She became something he found boring. And sure enough, they stayed married and faithful into old age and death ... It was ever after, but it wasn't happy. He had manipulated and contorted Bea into something that desired him, but what a sad thing that was. And so, he twisted and contorted himself into something more desirable, but what a monster he had become. He no longer recognized Bea. When she was something that wanted him, she wasn't still something he wanted.

Sam tried everything he could think of under the sun. No kids, multiple lovers, terminal illness, he even tried making himself and Beatrice stepsiblings at some point. But it was all just as miserable. It seemed that the things he loved about Bea were the very things that broke his heart.

And Bea, when she was herself, seemed to Sam to be just not a very good person. He grew to despise her, yet he needed her all the more. And still he hacked away at it.

BARNACLES

Barnacles had spotted his book through his fishbowl while Chris was carrying him around, and after sufficient convincing, Chris pulled it from the shelves and sat down. It was an easy book to find; a huge, plasticky hardback, supplemented with graphics, like a school textbook on history.

"See here now, Mr. Chris, let us see how my contributions to science have changed the world, and if I'm to receive the recognition I'm due."

"You're a … science fish? Nothing surprises me anymore."

Chris helped the English-Fish read through his book, up to the end, where Barnacles read about his funeral. Barnacles had been a rather influential, well-educated entrepreneur. Not a small number of significant innovations were attributed to him. This was a fish with an incredibly gifted mind. But it would seem that his life was a small drop in the bucket of all technological advancement. Flags weren't flown at half-mast at his death, dignitaries didn't visit from around the world to attend his funeral, and his life's work culminated not in the bang that Barnacles had wanted, but a fizzle which he turned his nose up at.

"Well, it seems as though things hadn't quite taken off in my life as I had hoped, but I'm sure my two cents will be worth a pound when I'm dead."

But it didn't happen. Barnacles' own great grandchildren didn't know his name.

"No. I have certainly got to be remembered for something. This just will not do. Mr. Chris, be a good man and write something for me, yes? Yes, very good, see, we must go back and give me sole credit for my big discovery; my partner certainly hadn't contributed quite so much as me. I would have done very well without a partner, yes, and he certainly never would have done without me. Let's do away with him, yes?"

Chris rolled his eyes and did as the fish asked, crossing out Barnacles' intellectual partner, and crediting the work entirely to one man, or rather fish. After reading forward, this had the immediate effect of proving Barnacles' partner rather necessary to Barnacles, as the discovery had never been made.

"Preposterous, I daresay. What an absurd idea that is, that I wouldn't have come up with it on my own. Why, of course I would have. Oh well, Chris, good chap, I suppose you need to supplement something of this obviously defective book. Have my previous partner, umm, contribute to me inadvertently, as a friend, without officially working with me. I suppose we can let him give me just a little nudge in the right direction, if that's what I needed."

And now Barnacles had remade the discovery, and been credited with it solely, and indeed, his fame increased slightly. Chris thought that Barnacles really overestimated the importance of his discovery. And Barnacles was clearly unsatisfied. He asked Chris to give him a couple other accomplishments. He started with small things, like graduating Valedictorian, and became increasingly more ambitious. Re-writing history, so that it was Barnacles the fish that achieved some of society's most significant advancements. But he couldn't quite go down in the history books like he wanted. No matter what, it seemed, even his own posterity forgot him like a vapour in the wind.

"My intellect is just unappreciated, Mr. Chris. Men don't recognize genius when presented with it, and if ever they do, they respond to it with jealous bitterness. They should be making statues of me. Let us give them something that they cannot forget."

Chris didn't know why he went along with Barnacles' changes. Perhaps it was morbid curiosity. He enabled Barnacles to do drastic, twisted things in the realms of science and politics. Such extreme ideas, innocuous ideas when explained by Barnacles. "It's for the greater good, of course." Barnacles rationalized some truly abominable things which did, indeed, assure his place in the history books—as a villain. His grandchildren remembered him. They were ashamed of him. They made public apologies on his behalf. There were no statues of Barnacles, but monuments to his victims.

Barnacles chuckled. "Ha, and they still have no appreciation for it. They recognize my greatness but see how afraid of it they are! Delightful fools. They don't know what I did for them. See here, Mr. Chris, this is the fame I deserved, but it seems my genius was a bit too much for them to handle, now, isn't it? Ha, see them, Mr. Chris? They all, the lot of them, are like children to me …"

Chris backed away slowly in horror, leaving Barnacles there to monologue in his fishbowl alone, evil British cackles echoing throughout the halls of the Library.

CHRISTOPHER

Chris was shaken; Barnacles' sick laugh rang in his head. He didn't know what to make of it, and he hoped that the people that had been killed, had somehow only been killed in the book. He tried to put it from his mind and went on looking for his own book.

There were so many books, endless, and no two were alike. But they were all very intentional, purposeful, meticulous, artistic. They all had names specially laid into the spines. He turned corners and wandered halls aimlessly for a while. He couldn't decipher any organizational scheme that might help him find his own book. And then it was there.

Chris opened his book, and when he did, he knew that this whole thing was real. Well, maybe not real in the sense of causal events taking place in his universe, made up of matter and energy and following Euclidean geometry and Newtonian physics. He doubted that was the case. But this Library was real in that it was legitimate, valid, true. He read about things in his past that he had long forgotten, read details he couldn't have known, and saw connections he never would have made on his own.

"Now, let's see what sort of things we will set straight."

Chris had been wronged a great deal in his life. It seemed everyone was out to get him. Chris knew exactly what he wanted to change first. His uncle had left him, and only him among his cousins, out of the will, and he meant to rectify that. But he thought it would be prudent to first experiment with a smaller matter. (He was still quite shaken by the events he observed from Barnacles' story.) Perhaps appeasing his decades-long feud with his villain of a neighbor would be innocuous enough. It had gotten quite nasty—trash thrown over fences, trees poisoned, and even a lawsuit, in which, of course, the biased court sided with his neighbor, who had put on an incredibly convincing pity-party and innocence act.

Chris considered using his new authorial powers to burn down his neighbor's house, but then, he thought, he is a man of reason, and perhaps if he could only make his neighbor not be so inept and quarrelsome ... Chris pondered the things the librarian had said, and he thought, as he was a man of reason, he could satisfy both parties. It might be possible to go back and resolve the issue in its infancy. But then Chris couldn't help but laugh at himself upon realizing that he didn't remember what they had been fighting over in the first place.

"I suppose it might be worth investigating the book of my neighbor. Perhaps I ought to do that."

And so Chris did take his book and go to find the book of his neighbor's, so that he could set things straight. When he had found it, he opened up to the part where his neighbor moved in next to him—except it wasn't there. His neighbor had lived in that neighborhood since before Chris had. Chris felt sure that was wrong until he realized that he didn't actually remember his neighbor moving in. Only that for the first while there was no conflict, and he took no note of whoever had lived in that house. Prior to the conflict, Chris had assumed that a more peaceable person lived in that house. What had been the original source of contention then?

Chris discovered that the previous owner of his own home, who had passed away, was a dear friend of their neighbor. They had lived in those houses most of their lives, and they had each gifted one another trees, planted in each other's yards, right on their shared fence. Chris couldn't imagine why anyone would do such a sentimental thing. Chris had cut down the late owner's tree almost as soon as he moved in—a thing that deeply saddened his neighbor. It seemed as though Chris had been outraged at his neighbor's tree dropping pine needles in his yard. Chris had an *aha* moment as he finally remembered why he had hated his neighbor so much—that blasted tree was half in his yard. Chris responded by raking up all the pine needles and dumping them over the fence into his neighbor's yard. Then it came about that Chris began dumping other things into his neighbor's yard out of spite. Eventually, he sued to have the tree cut down. But as Chris read on—the book gave him a different perspective: his neighbor never wanted to go to court, he just wanted to keep his friend's tree. He had been willing to cut the branches or come over and rake the needles ... Perhaps the neighbor had been a bit daft about it, (he was dealing with the loss of his friend, after all) but Chris had been outright spiteful. A sense of guilt enveloped him as he read.

"Is this what it looks like from the outside?" he muttered to himself.

Chris had an intellectual grasp of the concept that there are two sides to every story, but this hit home for him. For the first time in his life, Chris stopped to consider— "maybe I was on the wrong side." He had always seen his neighbor as a bad guy in his story, only to realize that he himself was the bad guy in his neighbor's story.

A gut-wrenching conviction gave way to a sound resolve. Chris knew what it would take to make things right. He wrote an apology to his neighbor. He went back and replanted the tree.

"There. My debts are settled." Chris was pleased with his work.

Chris shook his head to move on and turned his attention to his uncle's will. He would make it fair. He only wanted his share, what was rightfully his. To change his uncle's will, he'd have to find his uncle's book. And so, he set out to do so. It took a good while (it was a big Library after all). Chris was especially shocked to see his uncle's name when he finally did—sure that it was the wrong book. The cover of this book was vibrant and playful, full of energy and life. Chris raised an eyebrow at how the book he held in his hand contrasted so drastically with the uncle he knew. He remembered his uncle as a hollow, shriveled sort of thing, with nothing much to do except be sick and die. But when he opened his uncle's book, he read about someone he had never really met.

There was no way that this was the right guy. Well, it had to be, but Chris was absolutely shook. His uncle Ronald had been in a traveling quartet—with a beautiful soprano. Music was his passion, but when he got sick, he couldn't sing anymore; so, he learned the piano instead. Chris had never even heard him play. As Chris read, he didn't read about the shrewd uncle he knew; he read about a sweet, caring old man who was stricken with sickness and discarded by his nephews. He read about an uncle that was used, someone whose value as a person was overshadowed by his value as a monetary asset. And how Chris was the worst offender of them all—and how, despite all of it, his uncle cared deeply for him.

Chris read about how Ronald had made the tough decision to not leave money to people whom he knew would be torn apart by it. Which wasn't Chris alone—Chris was shocked to learn that his cousin, his uncle's own son, received only the estate and a condition that it would never be sold—nothing in the way of monetary assets. And then Chris recounted that he actually *had* received things, a trust fund for college for his children if he ever had them, the piano (which Chris now regretted pawning), and some other small, sentimental things. Chris began to weep softly as he read.

He thought about what the librarian had said, and he decided to let it go. It was hard, letting go, admitting wrong, accepting defeat to his own goals ... But it was also so easy. Chris let out an audible sigh of relief as the immense burden left his weak back. He felt as though he could breathe easy now.

His whole life was like this. He had viewed people either as enemies to his goals, or as tools to be used by him to achieve his goals. Never had he thought of those around him as people, characters, equally as valid and deep as himself, with their own story, struggles, hopes, fears ... And so, for this, Chris repented—he went through his life and apologized and made things right. He didn't just undo the wrongs he committed; he took steps to appease. Where he had swindled, he repaid twice-fold; where he had lied, he confessed the truth; where he had destroyed, he rebuilt better. And when he had gone through his entire history up to the present—he thought to himself that he ought not go further. For he had everything he needed to see things differently now.

ELIZABETH

Elizabeth's book was elegant, Victorian era, a burgundy hardback with inlaid gold designs. She opened it to find meticulously hand-painted typography; you know, the kind of calligraphy where the very first letter of the chapter is twelve times too big and barely legible. She furrowed her brow because she felt as though this style of book was unfitting for herself. It wasn't.

Elizabeth was a mother. If any mother were handed a book such as this, one of the first things she would do would be to go back and savor precious moments which had been lost to time. A first and a last for everything, always bittersweet. First words, first steps, first time riding a bike—and a last time breastfeeding, ever, a last time her kids wanted to hear a bedtime story, a last time the family is all together for Christmas … There was a time in her life when she set down her eldest son to let him run off and play— never to pick him up again. Pictures only do so much. But reading her story, Elizabeth was able to really relive precious moments, reading about things she had forgotten or never even knew about in the first place. Going through these memories, she lost track of time; like one does when reading a good book. (By the way, don't forget to do that thing you have to do.)

Not all was pleasant; reliving certain events broke her heart now as they had then. So many times, her children asked for things she couldn't give them. Explaining to them that it wasn't because they were naughty that Santa Claus didn't bring the bicycles and iPads that other kids received. Assuring them that second-hand clothes were cooler than new clothes because they had character. Having to scold them for touching the thermostat because she knew that degrees meant dollars. And all the hard days and long nights—double shifts at the diner, overtime, second job at the coffee shop. Always juggling more than she could handle, always exhausted, always aching, always drained of energy. Memories fueled the fire inside her.

Sometimes it was easy to blame her children. If she hadn't gotten pregnant, she would have finished college, gotten a decent job, and been financially stable. Then she could have started a proper family. But Elizabeth had seen enough episodes of *Twilight Zone* to know that she dare not try to mess with what was most dear to her. She wouldn't trade her kids for the world. She just wanted a break. She just wanted to give her kids what she never had.

And all it took was the simplest change. The littlest thing. She didn't have to go into her bank account and add zeros, she didn't have to win herself the lottery. All she did was sway a job interview in her favor. Right out of her second year of college, when she first found out she was pregnant, she applied for a secretary position at a law firm, but never got a call back from the interview. It would have paid triple, been so much easier on her, and had nice benefits and security. That is all she did—one simple change to fix everything forever.

No one, she was convinced, had ever been happier than her, to read about herself being able to just … buy diapers, and not have to worry so much about it. She smiled to see herself being able to keep a full fridge and take a trip with her kids every now and again. Furthermore, as it would seem, the position in that law firm turned out to be a much better opportunity than she could have hoped. It was a gateway to send her back to finish college—and come back as a paralegal. She was able to buy a real house with a reasonable mortgage and give each of her kids their own bedroom. When her oldest was starting high school, she was able to take a break from work to go to law school. She didn't get to see as much of her kids for those years, but when she came back—she had a security for them that was like a financial burden burned away to smoke.

Now, it was the other kids who were jealous of her own. High school friends would end up asking their mom for a car like Elizabeth's kid had. There wasn't much left to want. Work became more demanding, and so did her children. One day Elizabeth came home early from a work trip to find her teenage son throwing an absolute rager of a party in her house. She was livid. Vomit in the hot tub, penises drawn on the family portrait, drugs, and garbage everywhere. So stressful.

And then Elizabeth stopped and wondered how it had come to this. In the Library, she sat up from writing in her book, tapped her pen on her chin, and wondered exactly how much money was enough. She had thought that she just wanted her kids to have what she never did, which is true, but more fundamentally than wanting her kids to have—she wanted to provide for them, and when her kids had, it so happened that they no longer needed from her, and it left her in an endless cycle of always striving to give them more and more. And the satisfaction of it all was completely lost in her simple acquisition of the thing by penning in omnipotence. She felt like how a baseball player would feel if you went to his house and handed him a box full of trophies that he in no way earned. She didn't want the stuff, she wanted to earn.

She went back to writing. Back to work.

LILY

Lily sat down cross-legged with her book in her lap. She ran her hand across the cover; it was hard bound in a dark cyan dyed flax canvas. Quite a pretty sort of oceanic deep blue-green, like the colour of her beanie. She carefully lifted the thickly woven, textured cover to reveal stocky, off-white pages, and beautifully typewritten courier font lettering. She gently turned the pages, reading about her childhood. Some things she remembered; some she didn't; some that she remembered differently.

"I don't know who would write something like this."

Lily took her pencil in her hand, a classic yellow #2. She would give changing things a test run. But on what? Then Lily found the perfect mistake to undo. When a child, Lily was given a lovely sea-foam green dress with swirly brown designs, reminiscent of tree branches, or maybe roots. It had belonged in her mother's childhood before her, held on to for decades to be passed down one spring Sunday when Lily was seven. She loved the green, but she wasn't so fond of the brown designs. So one day, her silly little self decided to try to fix the dress. She had learned in school that blue and yellow make green, and so she carefully mixed the paint—and began to cover the brown designs. But almost as soon as the brush touched the dress, she knew she had made a mistake. So, she remixed the paint to a better blend. She only got halfway through covering the brown before she knew she was in trouble. She tried washing it in the sink, which just bled the paint everywhere, she tried scrubbing it, which seemed only to set the stains worse. At a loss and in a panic, she turned to bleach, knowing only about it that its job was to unstain fabric. Before she had given up on saving the dress, it was a sopping, blotchy, foul-smelling mess. And so, she did the only thing left to do—she hid the dress under her bed, (which bleached the carpet, mind you). And when her mom found it, how Lily cried.

Rolling her eyes at her seven-year-old self, Lily began to re-write that part of her life. No more paint, no more mess. And to her delight, it worked. She wore that dress until she grew out of it, and it stays in her parent's house to this day, waiting to be gifted to a grandkid. Lily was happy, and ready to begin to make serious corrections to her life.

Still reading and writing, Lily cringed at some of the things she had done and said. She was mean to people she liked, and nice to people she hated. So painfully insecure. Lily couldn't help but be thoroughly surprised at how different she was year to year—day to day even. She had always thought of herself as a constant, the control in a system of variables, but it wasn't so. Lily wasn't as concrete a thing as she had thought. There was seven-year-old Lily, and thirteen-year-old Lily—neither of whom existed anymore, except for in the mind of present-day Lily. There was happy Lily and sad Lily and hungry Lily. There was the Lily that existed in her dad's mind, and the Lily that existed in her friends' minds, and there was the Lily that had existed in her own mind—none of which captured fully the same as the Lily she read about now. The Lily in this book was made up of many different ages, and decisions, and thoughts, and viewpoints and reactions to her circumstances, big and small … All of these things came together in a grand mosaic to create Lily, the character in the book.

After some reading, Lily came to the first day of her 8th grade—when she had cut her hair short! She shuddered reading it; it was painful to relive. The day before school started, she took clippers to herself in her bathroom, and it was bad. Short short, like a boy. There was nothing classy or fashionable about it. It was her attempt at opting out of the whole thing. She didn't want to carry the weight of wondering if her hair was as pretty as the other girls'. She was so afraid of being laughed at … that she made sure she got laughed at.

Gripping her pencil—she had at herself. No more haircut. She would be a normal girl. It was a rather small and simple change, but it made her very happy to see that her mom didn't yell and that her little sister didn't cry at breakfast that morning, Lily didn't receive any weird looks or comments at school … It was good. Until Lily remembered her dad sitting down to talk to her about it. Or, now, not.

She flipped around, looking for a conversation she knew wasn't there, but she wanted it to be there. If her hair had been cut, her dad would have come into her room that evening, despite her insisting that she didn't want to talk. And he would have brought hot chocolate. And he would have told her how beautiful she was, and given her a hug, and told her that she had nothing to prove to the people that loved her. He wouldn't have had to ask why she cut it, because he knew; he'd been a teenager once, too. He would have held her as she cried, and at the end of it, ran his hand through her short, hack-job of a haircut and offered to try to clean up the uneven spots. And they both would have laughed, then spent an hour trying on every hat in the house, until her dad dug up an old blue-green beanie …

Lily reached up to the top of her head. Her beanie wasn't there; it never had been there. She never cut her hair, and never had that moment with her dad. This saddened her, but she was sure that it would be fine. Things would be different, she would be different, but she would be better.

Lily continued on and changed things further. Re-wording things she said to be more clever, erasing clumsy, embarrassing moments and mistakes, until she was at the end of the 8th grade, and she had many more friends. But she also had many more worries; she found herself with new problems to solve. She got asked to prom by Andrew Davis, and she said yes, so she blew off her rebellious friends, who had all made a pact to ditch prom together. They would have driven around that night, being silly, drinking gas station hot-chocolate, talking about how prom was stupid and they don't need it. They would have sat at the reservoir and looked at the stars, listening to Radio-Head. Instead, she had a fight with them. They accused her of abandoning them for the cool kids. And she accused them of just being jealous, saying they would have gone, too, if anyone had asked them. Lily had to make a choice—she couldn't both go to prom and not go to prom.

Lily missed all these things. She wanted them to happen. She was afraid of who she was becoming. But still sure that she could fix it, she went on. She undid kisses she regretted, avoided fights she wished never happened, did things she was too afraid to do, said things she was too shy to say … But with every change she made came a cascade of consequences. She had never stopped to consider that butterfly effect thing she had heard explained in some internet video. But this wasn't that … Uncutting her hair didn't somehow lead to Soviets ruling America—instead the effects were direct, connected. Not cutting her hair led to her dad not giving her a hat; going to prom meant blowing off her friends; becoming popular meant she didn't have any time for Fredrick Dinkle, and so he never gave her a lily stem on her birthday; not spilling mustard on her shirt that one time led to her missing out on that tiny shred of humility.

Lily began to panic. She was making a mess of her life. She couldn't even remember what she had been so eager to change—why she felt the need to mess with it.

She tried to change certain things back; she tried to add things to regain what had been lost. She even went back and tried to make sure that the green dress was ruined again, or that Freddy's flower got smushed. Reality blended with her lies until the two seemed homogenous to her. Her whole past was changed, and her whole future would now never happen. She lost track of time, and became incredibly frustrated as she worked in a panic, until all of a sudden, she caught a glimpse of her own blonde hair and stood up. She was taller now, and dressed differently, but what horrified Lily most was that she was arrogant; she wasn't close with her family or friends; she cared so much about what people thought; her quirks and passions and all the colours of her personality were smudged into obscurity, she had become a thing she didn't recognize. And, she thought, a decidedly worse thing. Lily was dead and gone. The thing standing here was, it was, a sopping mess. She felt like her seven-year-old self, playing with paint and bleach.

8

IT'S THE CHARACTER
THAT MAKES A STORY

C HRIS AND THE LIBRARIAN sat a ways off and
watched the people toil and curse their books.
Chris asked the librarian why they couldn't write what
they wanted.

"They can. They're all writing and getting exactly
what they ask for."

"Then why are they so … hopeless?"

"Would getting what you want always make you
happy? Is a hopeful child one that gets to play in the
street and always have ice-cream for dinner?"

"But look, she's not an evil person; she's trying to
write herself to be better … Why isn't it working?"

"When someone writes in their book, they can
change anything. They could give themselves superpowers

if they wanted, or give themselves terminal cancer at seven. But what they can't change with that pen of theirs is themselves. Jane's story is a sad one—not because of anything to do with the plot, or the setting it takes place in—but because the main character is sad. She is vain, and a vain person will be a vain person no matter what world you drop them into."

"Why couldn't she just write herself to be not vain—just write that her character has humility? Why don't they write themselves to be at peace?"

"How can they write peace when they don't have it? She cannot write humility because she doesn't know what humility is. A writer must be wiser than his characters. A good story requires a good author."

"Yes. We all ought to make peace with the lot we're dealt."

"Well, you're supposed to stop caring so much about your lot. If that's all you can see, then you'll never be happy, regardless of what your 'lot' is. You'll never be able to see the story if you're too busy grumbling about your place in it. If you choose to hate the snow, you'll have less joy in your life, but the same amount of snow."

"Is that why you didn't alter your own book? You realized that one can never achieve happiness if they're consumed with its pursuit?"

"It's a paradoxical ordeal, really. There was this guy in my group that felt ignored, misunderstood, unseen, unimportant … All he cared about was attention. He was so concerned with being heard, it was eating him up … But when he finally started to listen—his value shifted. He found happiness. He changed; he didn't need to be heard anymore. And ironically—this turned him into the type of person that people wanted to listen to. Only when he made peace with where he was did he make it to a different place."

"And we really need suffering and despair to get there?" Chris struggled to swallow it.

"Despair is a state of mind—our reaction to adversity, struggle and pain. No, we don't need despair, but we do need adversity. You're made to fight for something, and work towards something, and push the limits, and in the absence of that purpose, you can get pretty lost pretty quick."

Long silence.

"Chris, I want you to be the next librarian. You've seen what you were brought here to be shown; now it's your turn to help the next group."

"I don't know if I'm ready for that."

"I wasn't ready for it either. But you don't have to be anything special, just let the Library do its work."

The librarian handed Chris her librarian's due-date stamp.

"What is this?"

The librarian shrugged. "I don't really know; I think it's what made me the librarian. Stories are supposed to have symbolic objects. It might be important later, if ever we get a sequel."

Chris nodded, accepting the token, and the librarian stood up.

"I ought to go check on Lily now. I'll see you on the other side, Chris."

9

AUTHORIAL INTENT

S OBBING NOW, Lily ran to go find somewhere to hide herself. Tears splattered onto the book in her arms. Her mucky destiny swam in her head. She tried crawling under a desk and shrinking into nothing. She wished she was just completely buried. The librarian walked over to her sympathetically.

Lily cried, "Librarian, please help! I want to undo it all. Take it back. I can't write my own story. I don't want to. I've killed myself …"

"I can't help you, Lily. I'm the librarian, not the author. I didn't write your story; I don't know how it's supposed to go."

Lily got smaller, and her head sunk to the floor in defeat.

"I don't know how it's supposed to go, either. I don't know what kind of author would do this ..."

And as Lily spoke in her darkness, well, I wrote myself in to talk to her. You read that right—I wrote myself into my own story. And I said, "Hi Lily, it's me, Hunter. I wrote you. I'm your author ... What's so wrong with the story I made?"

Lily sniffled, sure of her own death. I knelt down under the desk with Lily. She answered "I, I just wanted the story to have a better main character. You made other people so, so, so much better than me ..."

I smiled to her. "Better how? Don't you know what makes a character a good one? Lily, I wrote with purpose, not on accident. I see more than you know ... To me, you're just words—something I took from inside my mind and heart that I put onto a page. If I'm a solid object, you're like my shadow. You're my poetry, Lily, and I love my poetry; in a way, it's a part of me. Do you understand?" (Of course, she wouldn't quite understand yet, because I haven't written it to be so.) She stared at me blankly.

"You're trying to tell me ... I'm not ... real?"

"No no no, of course you're real! You're real inasmuch as you understand the word. People think of real in binary terms—something is either real or fake—but it isn't so. A thing can be not as real as another thing, but still be quite real itself. You can feel the tears on your face, and the carpet on your fingers, can you not?" (And Lily could, indeed, feel those things.) "But what you cannot do is remember your mother's maiden name; I haven't bothered to write that yet. You also have a really vague, non-descriptive sense of what menstrual cramps are like. But that doesn't make you not real—you are real! You're full of emotion and thought—my emotion and thought. You're made up of parts of me and parts of others. People like you, that people like me have written, have toppled governments, inspired art, spawned whole universes, saved lives … You might not be as real as I am, but you have an actual impact on people that you can't fathom, and your life has every bit as much meaning as you hope it does, more so, in fact, than you could imagine."

I winked.

"Here, let me show you something. I'm going to give you supernatural knowledge, a little glimpse from outside your plane of existence, because I can. Here."

I touched Lily on the forehead, and her eyes went open. She had been blind, but now she saw. She saw more than you or I can see. The entire Library, the whole thing. An immeasurable web of intricacies, pages overlapping from books, sections, series. In the scope of the Library, the explosive power of a supernova was dwarfed in comparison to the explosive power of oxygen and hydrogens combusting to form a singular water molecule. The fall of a leaf from a poplar was every bit as epic as the fall of Rome. Every particle of dust dancing in the sunbeam was as steered as the stars in their courses. Lily saw it all. She even saw someone, bigger than her, like her author, reading this book now, experiencing her story. For a brief moment, somehow, her author had crammed it all into her small paper brain, or perhaps found a way to make her brain less papery. Lily saw why shrimp existed. She saw how the whole system of reality hinged on a handful of mathematical principles; she saw the angles and the ratios. She saw the artwork in it. Like reading a book about a rainforest one moment and standing barefoot in the Amazon the next. Her mind was stretched down to the black depths of the oceans and up to the expanse of the heavens. She saw herself, and she was so small and temporary. She laughed out loud, and tears filled her eyes. In the Library of everything, her personal drama was not near so dramatic as the epic multi-generational war between her immune system and the invading army of Staphylococcus bacteria that she ingested in a ham sandwich. It was all an absolute carnival. Bushes that turn sunlight into raspberries, reptiles that change colours. The sky didn't have to be blue, but it was, it was assigned blueness, and we loved it for that. The flowers weren't raised in the spring by automatic necessity; they, each and every one of them, chose to come up every year to do the job they loved, and they were good at it, perfect for it, actually. It was all one big poem, and also one big clock, and also a whole colony of miniature infinities. So much bigger, and also so much smaller, than we could ever comprehend.

"I am insignificant. I have spoken of things I don't understand. Things too wonderful for me. I was a character in your story."

"What do you mean 'was'?"

"I'm not dead?"

I laughed heartily, "Sorry, friend—I'm not done writing yet."

And then Lily awoke to find her same old self returned as she had been, all except for her eyes.

10

SONDER

LILY AROSE FROM THE Library floor with vitality, because she felt reborn. She had that freshness on her face and in her heart that one reaps after sowing a good cry.

"I understand now."

The librarian laughed. "Really? I don't think I do."

"Well, I mean, I think at least I know why he brought me here."

"Well, I told you that at the beginning, silly. To show you something. The Library gave you all the opportunity to play god, and make everything in your life exactly how you've always wanted it, down to your every whim. And what it's to show you is how much you suck at it. The things you think would make you most happy end up making you most miserable. The thing you think is the most horrible affliction is actually the most gracious blessing."

Lily nodded, because this was true. As she looked left and right, the bookshelf beside her was brimming with narrative. Every page of every book begged to be read, studied, laughed at, learned from. She pulled one out and opened it up.

"Aurelia. Born in Virginia in 1993 ... Tall, blonde hair ... Afraid of spiders ... Made a swing once all on her own in a tree she especially loved." Lily read on, and then her jaw dropped. "... met Evan at a train station when she was just sixteen and fell in love immediately."

This was the wife of that soldier! (Whose name, in case you've forgotten—as Lily had—was Evan.) Lily knew the astronomical odds of her finding Aurelia's book after having read Evan's in a totally different part of the Library. Lily pouted her lips.

"Hey, why did you leave Evan? You really messed him up." As though the book might speak back to her.

Lily, now thoroughly invested, bore into the book to find stories. How Aurelia left her affluent family in Virginia to elope with Evan and live in Massachusetts with him. The story of when Aurelia told her husband they were pregnant. And then the really big fight when Evan was drafted, and how she refused to attend his send-off. The gut-wrenching tears that night— uncontrollable, agonal sobbing on her living room floor, clutching her pregnant belly, alone. When the baby died, she had nothing left—no friends, no family, and no husband … A tear trudged down Lily's cheek as she read.

This story was heartbreaking; she wanted so desperately to reach into the pages and just give poor Aurelia a hug. And then she remembered she could! Hurriedly fumbling her pencil, Lily stuck her tongue out from the corner of her mouth and began to write herself into the novel. She wrote how a short, friendly, neighbor named Lily knocked on Aurelia's door with a pie the day after the send-off.

"Hi, I'm Lily, I live just down there, I just wanted to come and say, well, I'm sorry I never welcomed you properly to the neighborhood. I heard that your husband was sent off, and, well, I can't imagine what you're going through. Here, I baked this …"

Lily began to smile as she watched the story on the page change before her eyes. Aurelia wiped a tear away and took the pie.

"That's awful kind of you. Please, come in, or, if you like, do you have time? To be frank, I'm starving, and I think I mean to eat this whole thing now."

They both laughed and talked. Lily wrote how she would make tea. How she and Aurelia would have a genuine conversation, Lily writing her words and actions in the margins of the book as though she were journaling or writing a pen pal real-time. For hours she lay there with the book open in front of her and poured love into Aurelia—speaking life into this very broken woman. She was so absorbed in it she didn't even notice the librarian standing behind her.

"There you are."

Lily jumped up, startled, and wiped tears of joy from her eyes.

"Oh hi. Sorry, uhh … I hope we're allowed to write in books besides our own."

With a mischievous sort of face, the librarian produced a glossy blue book from behind her back.

"Guess what?!?"

The librarian extended the paperback down to Lily, who looked at it with confusion for a moment, and then took it after it was shaken eagerly by the librarian.

"Look what you did."

What I did? Lily thought. And then she saw Evan's name on the spine! Her eyes went wide and she flipped to the middle of the book to find, to her absolute delight and awe, that Evan came home to a loving wife. They grieved the loss of their daughter together, but had many more kids. He never started drinking, he never joined the mob … The story was completely changed.

"But how? I don't understand?"

The librarian was giddy.

"You did it, Lily. You changed a story."

"So, I can change someone else's story, just not my own?"

"Lily, instead of trying to rewrite your character as 'good', you actually did a good thing! You should look at your book again!" The librarian giggled.

She did, and to her delight, her book was a better one. Not because the plot or setting were different, but because the main character was. She had come to be a character that saw her place in the story differently, and no shift in setting or plot could ever take her new eyes from her. She closed her book and looked up at the librarian.

"Are you ready to go home?" the librarian asked.

Lily nodded. "How?"

The librarian rolled her eyes, "The obvious only way to leave a magic Library."

And with that, the librarian pulled a book off the shelf and gestured to its vacant spot on the bookshelf, inviting Lily to look. Behind the book was a void and, as Lily got closer, she saw an infinite space and a hint of a blue glow. Lily pulled a few more books off the shelf to expose more of the spacial vacancy, revealing the Earth hanging on nothing in an endless black abyss, a view as though she were standing on the moon. Her world seemed so small and far away, a rock floating in space, but also so close and personal—even though she shouldn't be able to, she could see her town, and her house, and her parents in the kitchen, and even her cozy bed. She swept enough books off the shelves to make a space large enough for her to fit through and was hit with a dreadful sense of vertigo, as though she might fall down forever into the nothingness. She stepped back and held onto the librarian for safety.

"It's okay, Lily, you just have to take the leap." Lily nodded her understanding and approached the portal with bravery.

"Lily ..." Lily looked back at the librarian, who was holding out her hand expectantly, "You can't take that with you," gesturing to the pencil in Lily's hand.

Lily held her pencil up and considered it. "I can't come back, can I?" The librarian pursed her lips. Lily put the pencil in the librarian's hands and nodded her acceptance.

The librarian was then surprised by a great and aggressive hug from Lily, "Thank you so much for everything."

The librarian teared up a little and patted Lily's beanied head. "Of course, kiddo. You'll be alright." When they separated, Lily backed up to the hole in the Library shelves and prepared to let herself fall.

And then Lily went home to be a good character. My character.

ACKNOWLEDGEMENTS

I HOPE THE INFLUENCE of Christian literature is apparent. C.S. Lewis, G.K. Chesterton, John Piper, Charles Spurgeon, or especially any reader of N.D. Wilson, all of whom I have in one way or another referenced the work of. If I were to have any one aspect of my writing shine through, I think I should want it to be Wonder—wide-eyed, childlike Wonder at God's great universe.

I cannot not acknowledge the fact that this story began as a seedling from a writing assignment in Ms. Arhart's English class. I owe many of my character ideas to my fellow classmates. I of course would like to thank my friends and family without whom none of this would be possible. My parents, brother Gage, Gina, friends Micah, Macxx, Spencer, Bubba, and Jason, cousins and grandparents all put in the time and effort to reading my book and giving me feedback and support, and a special thanks to my aunt, Connie, who went through many cups of coffee exploring these ideas with me. And Paper Angel Press, for being willing to invest in this absurdity sandwich of paper and ink.

Finally, I would like to thank the moon in the daytime, for making me feel like I'm on a planet, floating in space.

ABOUT THE AUTHOR

Hunter Terrell is a writer, artist, and adventurer hailing from the rugged terrain of Wyoming. He is a passionate Bible student, and a veteran who served in Afghanistan with Army Medevac at a young age. Along the way, he also completed his Associate of Science degree and became an EMT, with plans to continue his education.

When he's not scribbling down his next story or painting along with Bob Ross, you can find him exploring the great outdoors, hanging out with his awesome family and friends, and engaging in lively debates about storytelling, philosophy, and theology.

YOU MIGHT ALSO ENJOY

MODUS PERFECTUS

by Elisabeth Hegmann

Lonely misfits face foes, beasts, and their own inner demons in search of a mythical land of music … and end up finding themselves instead.

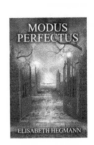

MAZES OF THE MIND

by Mike Sharer

Saxon knows something. People are desperate to know what he knows. But Saxon doesn't know what he knows. Only Kafka can help.

SMITH

AN UNAUTHORIZED FICTOGRAPHY

by Jory Post

In this kaleidoscopic joy ride of interviews that may or may not be real, of "ordinary" people who turn out to be anything but.